613

Lewin, Michael Z.
Family business.

| DATE | | | |
|---|---|---|---|
| | | | |
| | | | |
| | | | |
| | | | |
| | | | |
| | | | |
| | | | |
| | | | |
| | | | |
| | | | |
| | | | |
| | | | |
| | | | |

Other Books by Michael Z. Lewin

# FAMILY BUSINESS

## Michael Z. Lewin

A Foul Play Press Book

The Countryman Press, Inc.
Woodstock, Vermont

# 1

It was rare for Angelo to approach a family meal with trepidation, especially a breakfast. But his fears were confirmed when Rosetta appeared in the doorway. Angelo could see the trouble in her eyes.

It was a normal breakfast until then. Or was it? How often did David and Marie stay at table instead of scrambling for schoolbags, books and completed homework? And how often did Mama and the Old Man come down to join the rest of the brood for breakfast? Not often.

Coincidence today? Or did everyone want to witness whatever was to take place between brother and sister?

'I think I can hear Rosetta in the bathroom,' Gina said, warning her husband of approaching trials, as good wives did.

'I'm leaving,' Angelo said.

The adults of both generations understood this to be a feeble joke. David and Marie were less certain until they saw their father reach for another piece of toast.

Gina passed the honey.

'Thanks,' Angelo said.

'Cheer up, Dad,' David said. 'Worse things happen at aquariums.'

The Old Man frowned. 'What's at aquariums?' he asked. When nobody answered he turned to his grandson. 'What's at aquariums, David?'

David, who had merely been playing with words, was saved by his Aunt Rosetta's arrival.

Rosetta with the eyes. Focused solely on her brother. 'Well?' the eyes said. 'Well?' Rosetta said.

'Sit, Rose. Eat,' Mama told her daughter.

Obediently the twenty-nine-year-old Rosetta sat in her chair. But she was not deflected from her purpose. She said, 'I'm not hungry, Mama. I want to hear what Angelo has to say, now he's had his night to sleep on it.'

Angelo felt the family turn to him, as he'd known inevitably they would. He picked up a knife and rearranged the honey on his toast. He cleared his throat. He said, 'Well, Rose, I think – no, I'm *sure* I understand everything you say. Last night I went through it all again.'

'But you're still against it,' Rosetta said.

'Yes.' There. He'd said it. Angelo put his hands up in front of his face, as if defending himself. No one laughed. Rosetta's eyes screamed at her brother across the breakfast dishes.

'I'm sorry!' Angelo said. He continued, tapping the table with each syllable. 'It feels a wrong set of changes to make. It *feels* wrong.'

'No changes, he says?' the Old Man said. 'Is this the same boy who couldn't wait to reletter the office door when I retired? Who couldn't wait!'

'That was different, Papa,' Angelo said.

'Of course, different. God protect us from I should say something sensible. Huh!'

'How are you this morning, Grandad?' Marie asked. 'Is your cold better?'

The furrows above the Old Man's eyes became rainbows as he turned to his granddaughter. 'Better the cold, yes,' he said. 'But now I'm not sleeping so well, and at my time of life . . .'

'Eat your cereal,' Mama said. 'You don't want to be hungry at the solicitor. They don't serve food at a solicitor.'

'I'm eating, I'm eating,' the Old Man said. He picked up his spoon.

'So, you're seeing the lawyer today,' Angelo said, eager to peer through any window that might open on to an alternative conversational landscape.

'Unless he comes to his senses,' Mama said.

'It's my will,' the Old Man said. 'She wants my money on paper.'

6

'If you believe that . . .' Mama said.

Rosetta slapped the table. 'Don't change the *subject*.' The sharpness of her voice was uncommon at a Lunghi meal. The slap was unprecedented. Angelo felt it personally, as if she had slapped his cheek. Rosetta drew all eyes. Her own eyes aimed at her older brother. She said, 'The *real* reason is because it was *my* idea. If it was your idea it would be all right. I don't think Papa's wrong. I think Papa's right.'

'Suddenly I'm right about something,' the Old Man said. 'I can die in peace.'

'It's not that, Rose,' Angelo said.

'What then?' Rosetta asked.

Angelo's palms opened to the sky as he sought words for his feelings. 'This . . . What we have . . .' He looked from face to face, from generation to generation around the table. 'It's a family business, like a corner shop. Friendly. Papa started it that way, and that's how it's always been. It's a personal service we give. They come to the office, we make tea, we talk weather. We only talk business when they're ready. Then they tell us the problem, and we give satisfaction if we can. We work, they pay. It's the kind of business that everybody understands.'

Angelo paused, but only Rosetta's unrelenting face spoke in silent response. Angelo said, 'I said yes to the fax machine, right? I said yes to the photocopier. A computer in your office for the accounts? Of course! Makes sense, no problem. But to have computers everywhere, big computer eyes, blinking all over . . . Even in the office in front of the clients . . . To me that's a whole change in our style, a change in how we do business. And to me it feels wrong, Rosetta. It just feels wrong.'

'My old computer is slow,' Rosetta said. 'It's inefficient and a waste of time, *my* time.'

'Get yourself a new computer, no problem,' Angelo said. 'One super-quick.'

'It makes no sense to go half-way,' Rosetta insisted carefully. 'Why should I have to walk all the way to the office to get handwritten case records? Why should you have to walk to my room to give me messages or ask for an invoice? We *need* to be more efficient. We *need* to have linked terminals. We *need* a complete, modern computer system.'

'And where does it end?' Angelo asked. 'Terminals in the kitchen, in the bathroom? A terminal on the sideboard in the dining-room so when we talk business over dinner you can "access" the records from your chair?'

'Don't be stupid,' Rosetta said.

'I don't think I am,' Angelo said.

Rosetta glared at her brother. Angelo began to eat his toast.

Two people at the table were the family's peacemakers, its lubricators. When it was clear that Angelo and Rosetta had exhausted their own capacities for compromise, one peacemaker, Mama, appealed to the other. She said, 'Gina, you meet clients too. What do you think?'

Gina was silent for a moment, running a finger over her lips as Angelo and Rosetta turned to her. Then Gina said, 'I think if Rosetta says we need this equipment, then we need it.'

Rosetta was surprised to hear such unequivocal support from her brother's wife. She said, 'Thank you for that vote of confidence, Gina.'

Mama said, 'All right. Good.' She turned to her son.

Thus unexpectedly confronted by mother and wife, Angelo shrugged. It was acquiescence.

The matter was settled.

Marie felt freed to say, 'Well, I think computers are yukky.' She got up to look for her school-bag.

The Old Man, preoccupied, turned to Mama and said, 'What time again for the solicitor?'

David, Marie's younger brother, had not contributed to the substantive discussion. But his silence did not reflect disinterest. For David home access to a modern multi-terminal computer network with its mice, modems and megabytes represented nothing less than heaven on earth.

David had followed the tides of the negotiation with acute attention. He had despaired when his father declared himself against Aunt Rosetta's promised land. But when his mother made her unexpected intervention David's faith in the power of agnostic prayer was renewed. With the matter now settled

David could express his feelings. He punched the air with a fist and he said, 'Yes!'


At nine Angelo and Gina went through to the office as usual. It was their first private moment since breakfast. Gina spoke first. She said, 'Don't sulk.'

Angelo settled behind his desk. He rubbed his hands together. He sighed. He opened a drawer and took out a pencil and a notebook. He caressed the pencil. He stroked the notebook. Then he looked up to see if Gina was watching. She wasn't. 'I'm not sulking,' he said.

Gina prodded the soil in the plant pots on the sill of the window which overlooked the street. She knew the plants did not need water, but it was a way of passing time while she waited for Angelo to find a way to express his displeasure.

Angelo said, 'I'm surprised, that's all.'

Gina turned to her husband. 'At who?'

The question was unexpected because Angelo thought *that* was obvious. 'At you, of course.'

'At me?' Gina said.

'You didn't hesitate. Not even "either-or". Just "I think".'

'You ought to be surprised at Rosetta,' Gina said.

Angelo considered this statement but couldn't work out what she was getting at. 'What do you mean?' he asked.

'When was the last time you saw Walter?' Gina said.

Now Angelo was really confused. 'Walter? What's Walter got to do with this?'

Gina brushed specks of dust from the leaves of the scented-leaved pelargonium.

Angelo tried to find the link he was missing. Walter was Rosetta's long-standing, though married, 'boy' friend. But . . . 'I thought Walter was away,' Angelo said. He couldn't remember what he had been told. 'Business?'

'It's been more than three weeks.'

'Business can be three weeks.'

'Rosetta is obviously very upset,' Gina said.

'Is she?' Angelo asked. He searched his memory again, but

found nothing. 'What, has Walter gone back to that wife or something?'

'I don't know,' Gina said. 'She doesn't talk about it.'

Gina and Angelo looked at one another. Each knew that Rosetta normally talked to Gina about Walter a lot. But Angelo's face wrinkled. 'I still don't see what Walter's got to do with new computers.'

'You tried to compromise with her,' Gina said. 'You said of course she could have a new computer for herself if she needed it.'

'No thanks I got,' Angelo said. But he was beginning to see where this was going. It was not going to be about computers at all. He began to feel better.

'But,' Gina said, 'for some reason getting this equipment is very important for her. I mean, to pound on the table!'

'What reason?'

'I don't know,' Gina said. 'But that's why I said she should have it.'

'Because you don't know why she wants it?'

'Yes.'

'Oh.'

'And even if the new terminal's on your desk, we can still talk to people by the plants like we always do.'

Angelo looked across to the comfortable seating in front of the window which overlooked the street.

'And maybe new computers will save money in the long run, like she says,' Gina said.

Angelo shrugged, assuaged but not convinced.

At that moment they both heard the outside door open at the foot of the office stairs. Gina said, 'Fortune, maybe, knocking at our door?'

They both heard footsteps, climbing. The sounds were not loud. Angelo said, 'A woman. Seven and a half stone. Size four shoes. Left-handed. Recently returned from Copenhagen. What do you think?'

Although normally she would only have smiled, Gina laughed aloud.

Angelo located the pencil and notebook on the surface of his desk. Then he tried to visualize a computer sitting on it, a dominating, winking screen. He shook his head and rose to fill the kettle with water for tea.


The new client was indeed small and a woman. But Sherlock Lunghi had not predicted her prominent brown eyes or that she was in her mid-thirties or that her name was Eileen Shayler.

'Sugar?' Angelo asked.

'No, ta very much, Mr Lunghi,' she said.

Angelo carried three mugs of tea to the low table by the window with the plants. 'Biscuit?' he asked.

'No, ta very much,' Mrs Shayler said. 'Can we get down to business?'

'Of course.' Angelo sat next to Gina on the settee.

'It's my husband,' Mrs Shayler said. 'Jack.' She leaned forward to watch Gina add the name to the details she'd already recorded in her own notebook. 'He's in trouble. I'm sure of it.'

'What makes you think that?' Angelo asked.

'The washing-up liquid,' Mrs Shayler said.

'The washing-up liquid,' Angelo repeated. Gina wrote nothing.

'You see, this morning the bottle was by the sink where I left it.'

'Could you explain the significance of that for us?' Gina said.

'After I washed the dishes last night I left the bottle of washing-up liquid on the surface to the right of the sink. It's only a small surface, the one on the right. It's between the sink and the cooker.'

'I see,' Angelo said.

'What with the both of Jack and I being right-handed we always use the small surface whenever we make something to eat.' Mrs Shayler paused before adding with emphasis, 'Or something to drink.'

'Right,' Angelo said.

'I went to bed about ten,' Mrs Shayler said. 'That's my normal time, unless there's snooker on the television. If there's snooker then I may stay up until eleven or even later.'

'But last night you went to bed at ten,' Angelo said.

'Jack came to bed at ten forty-five.'

'Is that his usual time?' Gina asked.

'Yes,' Mrs Shayler said. 'He watches the news, you see, but me, I read. Of course when there's the snooker then I don't read, because with Jack already in bed it wouldn't be fair to him. Oh, Jack will take a look at one of his magazines when he's in bed, but only for a few minutes. It's not a proper read. It's not like a book. I read books.' Mrs Shayler leaned forward again. 'Have you got that?' Am I going too fast?'

'It's fine,' Gina said.

'But the other thing about Jack,' Mrs Shayler said, 'is that before he comes to bed he always makes himself a hot drink, *always*.'

'So,' Angelo said, 'if you went to bed at ten last night, there was no snooker on television, right?'

'No, no snooker. Last night was a normal night. *But . . .*' Mrs Shayler said, raising a finger, 'this morning there was something that was definitely not as per normal.'

'What was unusual about this morning?' Gina asked.

'Now, you have to understand,' Mrs Shayler said, 'in the morning I get up before Jack. He wakes up at the same time as me, but he has a few minutes' lie-in. He says it helps him to think through what he's got to do later in the day. So me, I get up first. And I make a pot of tea.'

'And this morning?' Angelo said.

'I went in to make the tea as per normal,' Mrs Shayler said. 'And what do I find, sitting there on the right-hand work surface, just where I left it last night? The bottle of washing-up liquid.' She leaned back in her chair and raised her mug of tea to her lips. But before she sipped, she nodded rhetorically, to underline the significance of her morning discovery.

Angelo and Gina took the opportunity to drink from their mugs too. Angelo even took a biscuit.

'That's a good cup of tea, Mr Lunghi,' Mrs Shayler said. 'Very nice, ta very much.'

'Thank you,' Angelo said.

'I think I will have a biscuit after all.'

'Please do,' Angelo said.

Mrs Shayler took a digestive.

# 2

That night, Tuesday, was one of three times in the week when a main meal was routinely prepared for the larger Lunghi household. Members of all three generations assembled for these occasions, which also took place Thursday evenings and Sunday lunchtimes. Among the diners this Tuesday was Salvatore, Angelo and Rosetta's older brother.

Salvatore was a painter and the only member of the family who did not live in one of the two connecting properties on Walcot Street. Salvatore was also the only one who did not live primarily on the income generated by the family detective agency. However, when he needed cash or the agency needed him, Salvatore too worked as a private detective.

The three big meals each week were occasions at which guests were welcomed. Salvatore's guests were always female though they rarely ate *en famille* more than a few times. Salvatore met a lot of women, but none, to date, had proved durable. This night his guest was an American who asked to be called Muffin.

'Muffin?' the Old Man said. 'What kind of name is a "Muffin"?'

'Why, an American name,' Muffin said sweetly. Her charming smile did its work.

'Nice,' the Old Man said. 'I didn't say it wasn't nice.'

'Don't badger the poor woman, Papa,' Salvatore said.

'Badger?' the Old Man said. 'What am I? Furry with a stripe?' He turned to Mama. 'He calls me an animal, this son of yours.' Salvatore's early decision to heed an artistic rather than an investigative calling left a residue of edginess between father and eldest child.

Mama's concerns about Salvatore were directed elsewhere. She wanted to see him married. Or at least paired. These were modern times, with things not like they used to be. Mama would settle for paired. But either way with Salvatore nearly forty he was definitely overdue. Mama ignored her husband and faced Muffin directly. 'So, dear,' she said, 'do you model for my Salvatore?' Most of them did.

But Muffin said, 'Oh my no, Mrs Lunghi. I couldn't possibly take off my clothes and then lie there without doing anything. I'm much, much too active for that. Aren't I, Sally?'

Salvatore smiled as Mama twisted uncomfortably in her chair.

Muffin said, 'Sally says I'm a natural human dynamo, but I wonder if the way I am isn't just one of those national things. Because just about all the American girls I know have given up on being passive. In fact, when I was sitting in that bar, that pub, what do they call it, Sally? The Green Tree? We were both in there having a drink and we didn't know each other from Adam but it was me that got up and came over and introduced myself.'

'Was it?' Mama said.

'Which maybe wasn't the way things were in your day, Mrs Lunghi, but it's the way all the girls I know at home are now. And I think it's great. So relaxed. So empowering.'

For a moment Mama gazed at her elder son, wondering how he would take to an empowered wife. Or 'partner'. 'Partner' would do.

Salvatore, however, had nothing to say to his mother on the subjects of Muffin or partnership. He addressed his younger brother. 'So what's new on the business front, bubba?'

'"Bubba"?' the Old Man said. 'Did I hear "bubba"?'

'We're getting new computers, Uncle Sal,' David said.

'Are you, now?'

'A whole network, aren't we, Auntie Rose?' David continued, speaking with enthusiasm of the brand of hardware and some of the new system's more salient qualities.

'Oh,' Salvatore said.

But Muffin was much more responsive. 'Why, those are just *great*, Davey. I wrote my thesis on one and it was about all I could do to keep my mind on the job and not use the other applications. You know what was neatest?'

'What?' David asked happily.

'It has the most *fabulous* graphics capability, just out of this world. I think my thesis was the only one that had little cartoons and designs on about every page. I wasn't supposed to put them in, but I couldn't restrain myself.'

'I think computers are yukky,' Marie said.

'Oh *no*, honey. They're just tools, like a sewing machine, or . . . or . . .' Muffin studied Marie to guess what she might be interested in. 'Or a CD player. They're all machines, but they can do *wonderful* things. I could show you if you like.'

'They haven't been delivered yet,' Marie said. She turned to her brother. 'Have they, slug-bait?'

'When will they come, Auntie Rose?' David asked.

'Day after tomorrow,' Rosetta said.

'So soon?' Angelo said.

'Don't start that again,' Rosetta said.

Angelo had not expected his remark to be jumped on. 'No no. I just wondered.'

'I should think *not*,' Rosetta said and then suddenly she rose from her seat. 'Excuse me,' she said and left the room.

'Is your little sister all right, Sally?' Muffin said in a whisper which everybody heard.

'Is she, Gina?' Salvatore asked.

'I'll go and see.' Gina rose and followed Rosetta.

'Anyhow, Davey,' Muffin said, 'when the hardware's installed I'd sure be happy to come over and take you through the software.'

'That would be *great!*' David said, immediately swamped by an image of himself at the keyboard and Muffin standing behind him, her arms around his, showing him applications . . . David found Muffin's lush mahogany hair and fresh complexion extremely attractive. Life was suddenly so rich as to be almost unbearable.

'And you too, Marie,' Muffin said. 'I'm sure you'll like it if you give it a chance.'

'Mega-yuk,' Marie said.

'Marie!' Mama said. 'Be polite.'

'Sorry, Grandma,' Marie said.

15

'Why, I'd bet ten of your pounds that if you give me an afternoon you'll end up saying, "I'd like to do more on this computer,"' Muffin said.

Marie opened her eyes and looked at Salvatore's non-model. 'Ten pounds? As in money?'

'Coin of the realm,' Muffin said. 'Or paper of the realm. Whichever you prefer. *If* you win. It's a bet, remember.' Muffin turned to the adults at the table. 'Is that all right? To bet with Marie?'

It was. Angelo said, 'The way to Marie's heart, offer her money.'

'It's not an offer, exactly,' Muffin said.

The Old Man laughed. 'Our Marie knows her own mind, young woman.'

'That's what I'm counting on, sir,' Muffin said.

Nobody understood what she meant. 'What does she mean?' the Old Man asked Mama. Mama's interest in Muffin had steadily increased, but she didn't know the answer.

Muffin said, 'I mean if Marie does enjoy the computer graphics I'm sure she'll be self-aware enough to say so.'

Marie had had a moment to consider. 'Is this a trick?'

'No trick,' said Muffin. 'You either like working on the computer and lose or you hate working on the computer and you win.'

'What happens if I lose?' Marie said.

Muffin smiled. 'So now you think it's possible that you might?' But she didn't push the point. 'If I win you will do two hours' work for me on the computer.'

'And if you lose you pay me ten pounds?'

Muffin extended her hand. Easy money was Marie's idea of heaven. They shook.

Mama felt it was her opportunity to ask, 'What kind of thesis?'

'Excuse me?' Muffin said.

'You said you did a thesis.'

'Oh. Right. Well, it was essentially a project on the mechanisms by which micro-organisms attach themselves to gut mucosa. Is that what you wanted to know?'

'I meant was it, say, for a teaching certificate?'

'A Ph.D., but that's pretty much the same thing.' Muffin smiled.

Mama said, 'You're Dr Muffin?'

'That's right,' Muffin said. 'But just the scientific kind.'

Mama looked from Muffin to Salvatore and back. This was not at all what she had expected from the early conversation. Indeed, Muffin was spreading much joy amongst the Lunghis.

'So do you have a paying job, Miss Dr Muffin?' the Old Man asked.

'Not at the moment, sir. I do have some offers in America that I'm considering, but now I've seen just how *beautiful* Bath is maybe I should look for something here.'

'Built on seven hills,' the Old Man said. 'Like Rome.'

'Have you seen many of the sights?' Angelo asked.

'Not in person, but I rode the open deck on one of the tour buses, and it was wonderful. The guide told us about the beautiful architecture, and how you had your own Master of Ceremonies from 1704 to 1761. An emcee for a whole city!'

'We had what?' the Old Man said.

'Beau Nash, Grandad,' Marie said.

'And the only hot springs in Britain, and all those Romans. I was going to check them out, but that's when I met Sally.'

'Fate,' Salvatore said.

'So maybe,' Muffin said, 'I'll go and ask for a job at your Bath University – they do teach something besides plumbing up there, don't they?'

Mama smiled at Muffin's joke.

'So you don't have a job?' the Old Man said.

'I've been working *so* hard for *so* many years that I decided to treat myself with a real fun trip. And so far, believe me, it's been just that.' She squeezed Salvatore's hand where it rested on the table. 'But I tell you, sir, I nearly wet myself when Sally told me that his daddy was a private detective. I *mean*, mine is a boring old rocket scientist, but to be a private eye! Well, wow! And that you have this whole business, with everybody a part of it. That's just a wonderful accomplishment to have.'

'You think that?' the Old Man said.

'Oh yes!' Muffin said. 'So, do you get called in to solve murders and stuff like that?'

To Muffin's surprise an immediate groan rose from around the table. She looked from person to person for an explanation.

'Well, since you ask,' the Old Man said, 'I did once work on a murder case.'

'Wow!' Muffin said.

'Norman Stiles was the victim's name.' The Old Man hesitated. David, who worked at his wit, laid his head on the table and covered his ears with his hands. Even Marie refused to meet her grandfather's eyes. 'But I've told it before and they don't like me to tell it again.' The Old Man leaned toward Muffin. 'Too gory,' he confided.

'Perhaps after dinner,' Mama said. 'You and the young woman can go to the library while I have a nice long talk with my Salvatore who I never see.'

Salvatore could see only too well what sort of nice long talk his mother was planning. He turned to his younger brother for relief. 'So what *have* you guys been working on lately?'

'There's been a lot of the usual,' Angelo said.

'So long as it pays,' the Old Man said. 'What's the complaint?'

'But,' Angelo said, 'this morning we got hired to work on the case of the un-missing bottle of washing-up liquid.'

# 3

The point which Mrs Shayler made about the washing-up liquid was that her husband Jack had not moved the bottle back to where it belonged.

'Every night I wash the dishes,' Mrs Shayler said. 'Normally I put the bottle in the cupboard beneath the sink. But sometimes, sometimes I forget. Well, we all do that, don't we? We're only human.'

'Of course,' Gina said.

'Ta very much. But because Jack and I have only the small work surface on the right-hand side between the sink and the cooker, if something's been left out it gets in the way for whoever wants to use the surface next.'

'So you're saying that when your husband went to make his hot drink before going to bed . . .' Gina began.

'The washing-up liquid would have been in his way. Exactly.'

'What's happened when you left the bottle out before?' Angelo asked.

'Jack puts the bottle under the sink where it belongs, and he comes into the bedroom and he tells me that I'm getting Alzheimer's disease. It's a little joke we have.'

'Yet last night,' Gina said, 'he neither put the bottle away nor said anything about it.'

'Exactly!' Mrs Shayler said. 'May I have another biscuit? I shouldn't, but I've been *that* upset this morning. I just haven't been myself.'

Angelo held the plate of biscuits for Mrs Shayler to choose and Gina said, 'Mightn't your husband have forgotten too?'

'Oh no,' Mrs Shayle said. 'Not Jack. Not something like that.' She picked up a Bourbon cream and leaned forward and lowered her voice. 'I suppose I must be completely frank with you.'

'That's certainly best,' Angelo said.

'Sometimes . . . Just sometimes, mind. Sometimes I leave the bottle out on purpose. Or the iron or a saucepan. I do it when he seems low and needs a bit of a lift. It never fails to cheer him up. Well, it's what a wife does for a husband, isn't it?'

'But last night was not on purpose,' Gina said.

'No. Strictly accidental. And I don't mean to suggest that Jack's low very often. He isn't. He's normally very . . . very *level*. And that's why what happened last night is so disturbing.'

'So what do you think actually happened?' Angelo said. 'Do you think that Jack didn't go into the kitchen to make his drink? Or do you think he didn't notice the bottle because he was preoccupied by something?'

Mrs Shayler leaned back with her tea mug in one hand and her Bourbon in the other. 'Oh, I did the right thing, coming to you,' she said. 'Everyone along the street says how clever you

19

people are. What good work you do for lawyers and all sorts. And I can see already that they haven't told a lie.'

'Thank you,' Angelo said.

'So, did your husband have his hot drink with him when he came to bed last night?' Gina asked.

'I've been worrying and worrying about that,' Mrs Shayler said. 'Ever since he left for work.'

'Did he leave at his usual time?' Angelo asked.

'Twenty to eight. Yes. He always leaves at twenty to eight. Jack is a very organized person.'

'And you didn't ask him?' Gina said. 'About the bottle?'

'Good heavens, no!' Mrs Shayler said. 'I couldn't possibly do that.'

Angelo and Gina waited for Mrs Shayler to explain further, but her silence made it clear that while one can consult private detectives about one's husband, *some* things are beyond the pale.

Finally Angelo asked, 'What does Mr Shayler do for a living?'

'He's an accountancy clerk. He's worked nineteen years for Whitfield, Hare and O'Shea. In The Circus? Do you know it?'

'No.'

'And every morning, rain or shine, summer or winter, Jack leaves the house at twenty minutes to eight and he walks to The Circus.'

'He walks?' Angelo said.

'Up the passage from Walcot Street to the London Road. Along the London Road, crossing at the lights, and then to Bartlett Street. Up Bartlett Street to Bennett Street and then left to The Circus.'

'Arriving at work?'

'In time to get himself settled before starting promptly at eight.'

'Excuse me for asking,' Gina said, 'but how do you know his route so exactly?'

'He always goes the same way. It helps him organize his mind for the day's work. I don't want to leave you with the impression that my Jack is never spontaneous or is a machine. But he does know what he likes. And he does know what he needs. And at the start of a new day he needs to be organized.'

Gina nodded and said, 'When you tried to remember whether he had a hot drink last night, what did you decide?'

'He had his mug as per normal,' Mrs Shayler said. 'Of that I'm certain. But what was *in* it, and whether it was hot, that I can't remember for the life of me.'

'I see,' Gina said.

'Sometimes I notice the little steams rising up. Or I smell the Horlicks if he's made his extra strong recipe because he's working on accounts for an important client. But last night, I simply don't recall, and I wouldn't want to make it up when I didn't really remember. To tell the truth I was so wrapped up in my book that I just didn't notice. I should have, but I didn't. I'm a bad and neglectful wife.'


'So what's the bottom line?' Salvatore asked. 'What put this guy off his stroke and made him leave the bottle out?'

'That's the critical question,' Angelo said.

'The critical question,' the Old Man said, 'is will she pay? An accountant's clerk? I hope you weren't soft-soaped by saying how clever you are?'

'She left a substantial retainer, Papa,' Angelo said.

'How much?'

'She left five hundred pounds.'

'Five hundred,' the Old Man said. He was not displeased. 'So where does she get this five hundred?'

'She works, Papa,' Angelo said. 'She paints ceramic cottages. Do you know them? The "quaint" cottages in the tourist shops?'

'These she paints?' the Old Man said.

'She does them at home. She saved the money for our retainer from that.'

'Cottages,' the Old Man said. 'They never get the colour of the stone right, the warmth. Huh!'

'But Dad,' David said, 'what are you going to do for her?'

'She wants a strategy that will find out what Jack's problem is.'

'The problem,' the Old Man said, 'is this wife doesn't have enough cottages to paint so she spends her time counting bottles in, counting bottles out.'

'She struck us as genuinely worried, Papa. And we've got to take the facts as the client presents them.'

'That's what you always say to do, isn't it, Grandad?' Marie said.

It was. The Old Man opened his hands. 'I'm a lucky man, my age, that some of my descendants listen to me.' Although he did not look at Salvatore everyone but Muffin knew that Salvatore was the covert subject of the remark.

Angelo said, 'Mrs Shayler thinks there's something seriously wrong, and she's willing to spend her money on it. So we assume there's something wrong.'

'But what?' David asked.

Mama said, 'It could be his work. Work can preoccupy a man. Heaven knows, I'm an expert.'

Angelo said, 'Yes. Maybe there's something upsetting at work, though Mrs Shayler says in the past he's never brought a work problem home.'

'Or he could be preoccupied, but by something else,' Muffin said. 'Is it all right for me to talk?'

'Why of course, my dear,' Mama said.

'Preoccupations *can* be about anything. And they don't have to make sense to anybody else. It could be something like . . . like he's seen a girl in a store as he walks past it. And this girl catches his eye once and she notices him looking, and waves, and now he waves to her every day and he even hangs around outside the window until she waves and gradually he thinks and thinks about her and now he can't control it any more and he thinks about her absolutely all the time.'

The detail of the hypothesis caught the adults at the table by surprise. Mama said, 'Do you possibly speak from personal experience, my dear?'

Muffin lowered her head for a moment. 'It's true. Something like that did happen in a lab I worked in. And it became embarrassing. Worse than embarrassing. But I wasn't bringing it up because it happened to me. I was just saying it doesn't need to be really important for something to upset somebody.'

There was a pause. Salvatore moved thoughts from Muffin's lab back to Mr Shayler by saying, 'It's a possibility – his problem could involve a woman.'

Angelo said, 'Distraction, preoccupation, that could be. But maybe what happened last night was that he didn't make his hot drink at all.'

'I don't understand, Dad,' David said.

'You don't understand anything,' Marie said.

'You explain if you're so smart,' David said.

'I would but you're too thick to take it in,' Marie said.

'Basta!' Angelo said.

Salvatore said, 'What are you saying, bubba? That the guy did something else when his wife thought he was making his drink?'

'That's it,' Angelo said. 'And then, because he needed to look like he'd made the drink maybe he filled his mug with water from the tap. That way he wouldn't have used the work surface, so maybe that's why he didn't notice the bottle.'

'So what's this husband doing instead of making his hot drink?' Mama asked.

'He might have met someone at the back door,' Salvatore said. 'Do they have a back door?'

'I don't know,' Angelo said. 'I'll find out.'

'Maybe he was making a telephone call,' Marie said.

'Good,' Angelo said. 'Your mum asked about the telephone and Mrs Shayler can't hear the phone being used downstairs if she's in the bedroom.'

'So who's he calling?' Mama asked.

'Has he got a girlfriend?' Is that it?' Marie asked.

'Back to women,' Salvatore said.

Angelo said, 'Possible.'

'Usually they go out for that,' the Old Man said.

'For what, Grandad?' Marie asked.

'Careful,' Mama said.

'To ring their fancy women. That's all I meant,' the Old Man said. 'Take it from me. A lifetime in the business. Suppose you see a man walk a dog. He stops at a phone box. He comes out smiling. That poor dog won't get much exercise. Take it from me.'

'Do they have a dog, Dad?' David asked.

'Mr Shayler might have made a late-night phone call from his house about something other than a woman,' Muffin said. 'Maybe he has money troubles.'

'Money troubles,' the Old Man said. 'That's more like it. He's up to the neck with a bookie. He gambles with clients' money. Or the stock market. Yes, this Jack Shayler sounds more like a money problem.'

Salvatore leaned to whisper into Muffin's ear, 'My father is obsessed by money.'

'What's he saying?' the Old Man said. 'What's he talking about me?'

'Salvatore, don't be rude,' Mama said.

'Sorry, Mama,' Salvatore said. 'I was agreeing about the money problem.'

'You have a money problem?' the Old Man said. 'Is that what he said? Work for a living, that solves it. Huh!'

'So what happens next, Dad?' David asked. 'Do you want me to tail Mr Shayler tomorrow morning? I could do it. It's only English first lesson.'

'We're not following anybody yet. But what do you think we *are* doing?' The question was addressed to David but with a sweep of his hands Angelo opened it to the rest of the table.

'Bug their telephone?' Marie suggested.

'Good,' the Old Man said.

'But not yet,' Angelo said.

'Someone small could hide in the house and watch him,' David said.

'Small brains aren't enough,' Marie said with a toss of her hair.

'Meet Shayler yourselves?' Salvatore said. 'Or go through their rubbish and see if you can find secrets on paper?'

'All this investigation is expensive,' the Old Man said. 'Five hundred won't last long. What does she say about when that runs out?'

24

'She says she'll pay whatever it takes,' Angelo said. 'And that she trusts us.'

'Spare no expense,' the Old Man said. 'Cottages. Huh.' He rubbed his hands together. 'All painters should make such money.'

Muffin said, 'Isn't this cloak-and-dagger stuff a little premature, Angelo, if I may say so?'

'Go on.'

'Well, it seems to me that your client is drawing a lot of conclusions from one tiny episode. I accept that she's the best person to judge whether the incident is important or not. But surely you and she need more information before you start tapping telephones or following people or sorting through the trash.'

Angelo smiled broadly. 'Exactly,' he said. 'Good. Good. Good.'

'So what *are* you doing, bubba?' Salvatore asked.

'Two things. Number one, this afternoon I rang Charlie.'

'A friend of the family,' Salvatore told Muffin, 'who is a policeman.'

'Charlie will run all the names,' Angelo said. 'But more important . . .' Angelo nodded to Dr Muffin, 'number two, tonight Mrs Shayler will leave the bottle of washing-up liquid out again. And she'll try to sniff her husband's mug.'

Salvatore turned to Muffin. 'There's nothing quite so glamorous as being private eyes,' he said.

# 4

Angelo was alone when he opened his office at nine on Wednesday morning. Gina, required as a witness in a Crown Court trial, had driven to Bristol immediately after breakfast.

The previous night, in bed, Angelo had asked about Rosetta. 'So what's upsetting her?'

'We didn't talk about it,' Gina said.

25

'Oh,' Angelo said.

'She went to the glass porch and sat looking across the river. When I went in she said, "Don't ask," so I didn't. I said, "May I sit with you?" and she said, "If you want," so I did.'

'That doesn't sound like Rose,' Angelo said. 'She's always so . . .'

'Deferential?'

'I was going to say "polite" but that wasn't quite right. Maybe "accommodating". But yeah, all right, deferential.' He paused to give Gina a chance to comment. When she didn't he said, 'What did you talk about?'

'She said she's bored to death cooking curries every Tuesday night.' Gina switched out the light.

Angelo said, 'It was her idea to change from pasta.'

Again Gina said nothing.

'You were out there a long time for talking curries.'

Gina rolled toward her husband. 'Well, first you chop the chicken, but you've got to have the marinade ready . . .'

'OK. OK. OK,' Angelo said.

'Rosetta's upset about her life. She thinks she hasn't achieved anything. Not like you and Salvatore have. By the way, did you ask Salvatore if he'll be available to work this week?'

'He said yes.'

'Good. And Rosetta thinks we don't value her, and that makes it all harder.'

'Don't value her?' Angelo said. 'We buy her computers whenever she wants them.'

'That's not what she means, and you know it.'

Angelo shrugged in the dark. 'What does she want to "achieve"?'

'It's not as specific as becoming a brain surgeon.'

Angelo considered. 'And what have I achieved, anyway?'

'Don't you start to curdle too. One at a time,' Gina said.

'I'll wait for you to call my number.'

'Rosetta *is* nearly thirty.'

'One foot in the grave,' Angelo said. He wiggled a foot. 'So you talked about her life, but not "it", whatever "it" is.'

'That's right.'

'So is "it" Walter?'

Walter was a conveyancing solicitor and had been Rosetta's friend, even fiancé, over a period of four years despite his married status. The situation was accepted because Rosetta was happy. The arrangement was so fixed, so permanent, that Mama had felt able to turn her pairing attentions back to Salvatore. 'Such sleepless nights he gives!' Mama said. For more than three years the pronoun in the familiar sentence had been masculine.

'It must be Walter,' Gina said.

'I suppose it has to be,' Angelo said. But neither had anything more to add.

Gina said, 'Did you talk to everybody about Mrs Shayler?'

'They think a bottle of washing-up liquid is the smallest problem we've ever had.'

'They prefer people dying?' Gina asked. Then, 'So how was Muffin?'

'She thinks what we do is "really neat".'


When he heard steps on the stairs Angelo guessed Mrs Shayler. Maybe a 'per normal' time to consult her detectives had already been established. So Angelo was surprised when the person who came through the door was his sister. 'Rose!' Angelo said.

'I'm not welcome? I'm part of this business, too, you know.'

'I was expecting the washing-up liquid.'

'I suppose,' Rosetta said, 'that Gina told you all about it.'

'She said you didn't want to talk about it.'

'I don't,' Rosetta said.

'So have a cup of tea.' Angelo moved to the kettle, which was already filled with water in anticipation of a visit by Mrs Shayler.

'No,' Rosetta said sharply. 'What will it solve?'

Angelo turned from the table with the tea things on it. He walked to his sister and engulfed her with his arms.

At first Rosetta tried to pull free but Angelo insisted and patted her on the back. 'I'm not your enemy,' he said.

After a moment she relaxed. 'Oh, I know,' she said. 'I know.' She dropped her head on to his shoulder, something she had not done for years.

They stood like that until Rosetta said, 'It's just that Walter went on holiday.'

'Did he?'

'With that *woman*. Who he says he hardly even talks to.'

'Oh.'

'And he didn't even tell me he was going to my face, Angelo! He sent me a letter. A letter, saying he "had to". That he "couldn't get out of it". Oh God. That's *so* pitiful. A *letter*!'

Angelo didn't know what to say. He said, 'How long is he away for?'

'I don't know!' Rosetta said. 'And I don't care!'

'Sounds like it,' Angelo said, and then wondered if his words would cause offence.

But Rosetta laughed and stepped away. 'You're such a comfort,' she said. But now there was no tension between them.

Angelo said, 'Did Walter give you no hint at all that he was going away?'

'None,' Rosetta said. 'Why?'

'It just doesn't quite sound like him, that's all.'

'How does a twisted, scaly, two-headed snake usually sound?'

'He's always seemed so, well, fussy about how things are done. Was this letter he sent handwritten or typewritten?'

At this Rosetta gave a snort. 'What are you asking? Did he write the letter himself? Was Walter kidnapped? I think you need some rest, Angelo. I think the job's getting to you.'

'Maybe. Maybe.'

'Take a holiday. Why don't you go somewhere? With your wife. Make another baby.'

'Can I afford it?' Angelo said.

'Not if you buy all that new computer equipment,' Rosetta said with a smile.

Angelo raised his eyebrows, but the computer thing was settled, there was nothing more to say. 'So, I can't make you tea. What did you come about?'

'There's a man,' Rosetta began.

'That was quick,' Angelo said quickly.

It was meant light-heartedly and Rosetta strove to take it that way, but despite her intentions she reddened.

Angelo saw, and Rosetta saw that he saw.

'Well, well, well,' he said.

Rosetta covered her face with her hands but then, knowing how that looked, she took her hands down again. However the colour was inescapable. She turned away, then she turned back. 'This is ridiculous,' she said. 'It's nothing. It's business.'

'OK,' Angelo said. 'What business?'

'A man is coming here to show you some equipment.'

'He's showing *me* his equipment?'

'Stop!' Rosetta said.

Angelo laughed.

'This equipment,' Rosetta persisted, 'is not computers.' She was about to explain what the equipment was when someone knocked on the office door.

'Maybe this is him,' Angelo said. 'Pink. It's a good colour for you.'

Rosetta moved to the door saying, 'He sells other things it might be good for us to own. He said he'd come today or tomorrow. I just wanted to let you know, that's all. I didn't get a chance last night. OK?' Rosetta opened the door.

Standing outside was Mrs Shayler. Neither woman expected the other. Rosetta was startled, but Mrs Shayler was frightened.

When Rosetta realized the visitor's fear, she took Mrs Shayler's arm and helped her into the room and on to the settee.

'Ta very much,' Mrs Shayler said. 'Oh dear. How silly of me.' She fanned herself with her hand.

'Are you all right?' Rosetta asked.

Mrs Shayler didn't answer.

Angelo said, 'Can I make you a cup of tea?'

Rosetta said, 'Angelo believes in tea-therapy, but I'll call a doctor if you want me to.'

Mrs Shayler said, 'I'm so sorry to intrude on your consultation. Please excuse me.'

Angelo said, 'This is my sister, Mrs Shayler. Rosetta's also a member of the firm.'

In a faint voice, Mrs Shayler said, 'How do you do?'

'Are you all right?' Rose asked.

'All right?' Mrs Shayler said. She lifted her hands to her face. 'My whole world is collapsing.'

At one o'clock Angelo locked the street door and crossed from the Lunghis' business building into the adjoining property that completed the family complex. Together the two three-storey buildings provided ample space for the household, even with the ground floor of each let out as a shop.

Angelo went to the kitchen to make himself lunch. As he did so he noticed the bottle of washing-up liquid sitting behind the taps of the sink.

Most Lunghi dishes were washed by machine now but the plastic bottle still sat on the window sill. Delicate china and things of awkward size and shape were hand-washed.

Sitting as it did in a convenient yet unobtrusive place, the plastic bottle did not seem to have the potential for malevolence or distress. Yet Angelo realized that even he sometimes used dish-washing liquid in acts of deception. Like when he washed a plate to destroy the evidence that he'd eaten something he didn't want Gina to know about. A last profiterole late at night, for instance.

Angelo's musings were interrupted by the telephone.

'Angelo Lunghi.'

The caller was Charlie ringing from the police station. 'We have nothing on either a Jack or a John Shayler at the address on Walcot Street or anywhere else in the city. And I went up to ask the fraud boys and girls about Whitfield, Hare and O'Shea, but it's not one of the accountancy firms they associate with dodgy dealings. They want to know if they should add it to their list.'

'Not as far as I know,' Angelo said. 'The name came up, that's all.'

'Pity,' Charlie said. 'So, are all these blanks I've drawn good news or bad?'

'Too early to tell,' Angelo said and then he asked Charlie about his family.

But Charlie said, 'I can't jaw-jaw. We've got a new bloke here

30

and he's got his beak into everything. Well, I say "new" but he used to work here and then he left. Thought we'd seen the last of him.'

'Is there something wrong with him?' Angelo said.

'Not if you like your CID detectives old-fashioned. But he hates computers, and he's suspicious of us who operate them. So I'm being careful for a while. If this bloke does decide to throw his very considerable weight around I want to make sure he lands on somebody else.'

'He's overweight?'

'I think that's fair to say.'

'So, how's his cholesterol?' Angelo asked.


Charlie's call was the only interruption to Angelo's lunch break. He had rather expected to see Rosetta, but she did not appear. And Gina's court case had clearly not been adjourned – as they often were.

Nor did Mama and the Old Man come down from their flat. Sometimes they came down and sometimes they didn't. Angelo never knew why each decision was made and he didn't ever ask. Thinking about it now, he became aware that it was rather like Mrs Shayler saying she couldn't possibly *ask* Jack why he hadn't put the washing-up liquid away. There were unwritten, unspoken rules. Every family had them.

After putting his lunch dishes in the dishwasher, Angelo crossed back to the office and went down to unlock the street door. There was nothing on the outside to indicate fixed opening times. As well as the agency name, the plaque on the door gave the telephone number. Little of the Lunghis' business came unannounced off the street. Most work came by phone and fax and most was from regular clients. Visitors to the office were common, but almost always they came by appointment.

So when Angelo unlocked the door from the inside, he was surprised that it was immediately opened from the outside. A man stood on the pavement. 'Mr Angelo Lunghi?'

'Yes.'

A broad smile filled the man's face. He was large, carefully coiffed and wore an expensive suit. About thirty-five, he sported two gold rings on his right hand. Angelo noticed the rings as the man extended his hand for a shake. 'Adrian Boiling,' the man said. 'Pleased to meet you. I believe your sister is the lovely Rosetta. She suggested I drop in to show you some of the best surveillance equipment you'll ever have the pleasure of examining.' In his left hand Adrian Boiling carried a large black sample case.

Gina appeared in the office a few minutes past four. 'He was fined a grand, got eighteen months suspended, and has been enjoined from coming within a mile of her or the kid or the kid's school. They all behaved so well you wouldn't believe it, which made for the most boring day I've had in weeks. How have things been here?'

Angelo began with Rosetta, intending it to lead, as it had historically, to Mrs Shayler. But the recounting of Adrian Boiling would not wait.

'I don't know what's taken hold of Rose's senses,' Angelo said. 'This Boiling talked as if it was a foregone conclusion that I'd have something off every page in his catalogue.'

'So what did you do?' Gina asked.

'I didn't buy anything,' Angelo said. 'But he pushed and pushed for me to test things. "We're sure if you try us you'll like us,"' Angelo mimicked. '"So we make it a company policy to offer free trials."'

'Of what?" Gina asked.

'Telephone bugs. Directional microphones. Compact tape recorders. Cameras. Concealed video recorders. Stuff kept coming out of his case. I suppose it proves just how micro the new equipment is these days. I expected him to produce a car that unfolded.'

'Poor Angelo,' Gina said, amused.

'I explained that we rent what we need, but Rose must already have told him that because he whipped out sheets of paper filled with numbers. Suppose this. Suppose that. He's decided we can't afford to do it the way we have since Papa began and

32

that it's a miracle we're still in business. Gina, what do I do? How could Rosetta get me into something like this?'

'What did she get you into?'

'He left a catalogue and an order form and his home phone number in case we want to ask questions out of business hours. He'll ring on Friday. He'll come back in person in a week. And we have a seven-day free trial of a telephone bug,' Angelo said. 'Because of Rose we're tapping our own telephones. And Adrian Boiling swears that once we've heard the clarity of the tapes, we'll never want to use anything else. It was excruciating.'

Gina cradled her tea and shook her head sympathetically. She kicked off her shoes and put her feet on the low table.

'Rose is my sister,' Angelo said, pulling the plate of biscuits away from Gina's feet and taking a rich tea in the process. 'What am I supposed to do?'

'Be careful what you say on the telephone,' Gina said.

Angelo dunked the rich tea resignedly.

'Tell me about Mrs Shayler,' Gina said.

'Ah,' Angelo said. 'Mrs Shayler.'

But before he could begin to report their new client's second visit, they both heard the street door open. Somebody ran up the stairs.

With a sigh Gina reshod her feet. Angelo stood up. The office door was thrown open. A flaxen-haired woman in her early twenties ran in. 'Is this the Lunghi Detective Agency?' she asked Angelo angrily.

'Yes,' Angelo said.

'Well, just what the hell do you think you're playing at?'


# 5


'She was beautiful,' Gina said. 'Slim, busty, a lovely tan and she looked wonderful in simple clothes, a plain white shirt and a full blue denim skirt. And she was *so* angry with your father that it gave her a kind of glow.'

Marie felt envious. David said, 'What had Dad done?'

'Well he *denies* everything, but he would, wouldn't he?' Gina said. 'Could you pass the butter please, Rosetta?'

Rosetta passed the butter silently, and waited for a chance to ask if Adrian Boiling had called in to see Angelo.

'My secret life,' Angelo said, spreading his hands. 'You try to keep all the women happy, but sometimes . . .'

'Dad!' David said.

'Wires get crossed . . . The women get cross . . .'

'*Dad!*'

'But she was gorgeous, wasn't she?' Gina said.

'I only take on the world's most spectacularly beautiful women,' Angelo said.

'What had Dad *done*?' David asked.


'What am I supposed to have done?' Angelo asked calmly in the face of the raging beauty.

'It's three pubs I know about for certain, and who knows where else!' the woman said. 'You've got no right! Already people are asking if I'm in some sort of trouble. They think I'm a criminal!'

'My name is Angelo Lunghi, and this is my wife, Gina. There's tea in the pot. Why don't you let me pour you a cup while you sit down and tell us what the problem is?'

'What's your name, dear?' Gina asked.

The angry woman seemed baffled by her reception. She said, 'Kit Bridges.'

'Pleased to meet you,' Angelo said. 'Do you take milk? Sugar?' He moved to the teapot.

'Doesn't my name mean anything to you?'

'Should it?' Gina asked.

'Well, if it doesn't, why have you been showing my picture in pubs? Why have you been telling people it's about something so serious you can't give details?'

*

'You've been showing her picture around?' David said. 'What case is it, Dad?'

'None that I know about.'

Uncertain whether his father was teasing, David said, 'Mum?'

Gina shook her head.

'But I don't understand,' David said.

'What else is new?' Marie said.

'You're so clever,' David said. 'What's it about?'

Marie looked at her brother disdainfully, but then saw that the adults were expecting her to speak. She said, 'Who's been showing her picture?'

'A man. In pubs,' Gina said.

'And he says he works for us?' Marie asked.

'He says he is a private detective,' Gina said.

Rosetta said, 'But we're the only detective agency in Bath.'

'Exactly!' Angelo said. 'And that is therefore making Ms Kit Bridges, part-time fashion model, conclude that the man works for us.'

'So who does he work for?' David asked. 'One of the Bristol agencies?'

'We don't know,' Angelo said.

'What pubs has he been in?' Marie asked.

'Three that she knows about,' Angelo said. 'The Rose and Crown in Larkhall, the Anchor off Kingsmead Square, *and* the Star.' The Star, at the top of Walcot Street, was the neighbourhood pub the Lunghis favoured.

'But he may have been to other pubs too,' Gina said.

'Why does he want to find her, this detective?' David asked.

'Ms Bridges says she can't think of anything a detective could possibly want to talk to her about,' Gina said.

'So she's not married?' Rosetta asked. Then blushed.

'No. Not even a steady boyfriend. She says she puts all her energy into her career.'

'Does she make a lot of money from modelling?' Marie asked.

Gina said, 'She must make some. The man has been showing a photocopy of a picture of Ms Bridges that was in a magazine.'

'And she's *so* gorgeous,' Angelo said.

'Dad!' David said.

'If she came to you, that means the detective hasn't found her,' Rosetta said. 'So how does she know he's looking for her?'

'She has a friend who works part-time behind the bar at the Rose and Crown,' Gina said. 'The friend recognized the picture, but didn't tell the detective she recognized it.'

'Why not?' Rosetta asked.

'Because he wouldn't say why he was looking for Ms Bridges,' Angelo said. 'Then today the friend and Ms Bridges had lunch together. When the friend told her about the detective, some people they were with said they'd heard that someone was looking for her too. That's how she found out he'd shown her picture in the other pubs.'

'If it were you,' Rosetta said, 'what kind of case would it be for you to show a photograph in pubs?'

'Good question, Rose,' Angelo said. He looked to Gina. He said, 'If we were looking for a drinker. Or a no-fixed-abode. Or someone who'd just moved here.'

'A runaway?' Gina said. 'Or a druggie. Maybe a fence.'

'A musician?' Marie said.

'Could be,' Gina said. 'But nothing that sounds like Ms Kit Bridges.'

'So what are you going to do?' Marie said.

'Do? Do? But who's the client?' Angelo asked, mimicking his father. 'So who pays? You don't run a business if nobody pays.'

Marie giggled.

'But,' David said, 'it's not good if people think this detective is one of us, is it?'

Angelo agreed. 'That's why we think we need to find out more about it.'

'Is there anything I can do?' Marie said impulsively, attracted by pubs and modelling.

'Like what?' Angelo said.

'I don't know,' Marie said. 'There might be something.'

'*She* thinks she could be a model,' David said. 'For horror comics, maybe.'

'Your father melted, *melted* when this woman said, "Oh, can you really find out what's going on, Mr Lunghi?" And you should see the smile on her. It was like a toothpaste ad!'

'I've always had a weakness for a good set of choppers,' Angelo said.

'Have you rung Salvatore?' Gina said.

'Not yet. I'll do it now.' Angelo rose from the table, but then he hesitated. He turned to Rosetta. 'We thought Salvatore might be happy to go out tonight and ask around for this detective, but if you'd rather do it, Rose . . .?'

'Me? Go to a lot of strange pubs?' Rosetta said. 'On my *own*?'


Meals on Wednesday evenings were informal and consisted mainly of foods that only needed heating. Eating was completed more rapidly than at the 'big' meals and David and Marie, in particular, usually left the table quickly. It was therefore not unusual that Rosetta should find herself alone with Gina. She said, 'Did Angelo mention whether a surveillance equipment salesman called into the office today?'

'He called,' Gina said.

'Oh,' Rosetta said. Then, 'Is Angelo buying anything?'

Gina said, 'Do you want us to buy something?'

'If you need something,' Rosetta said. 'I'm sure it's good equipment.'

'The salesman's a bit of a hunk, I gather,' Gina said.

'Is he?' Rosetta asked. 'I suppose he is, if you like them chunky.'

Walter was chunky. Gina said, 'Where did you meet him?'

'In the business computer shop. He runs that too.'

'Alan Boiling, is it?'

'Adrian,' Rosetta corrected.

'Have you gone out with him?'

'Of course not!' Rosetta said. 'It's nothing like that.'

'It's not illegal,' Gina said.

'We got to talking, that's all. I told him a bit about the agency and he mentioned the line of surveillance equipment.'

'Angelo says he spoke well of you. "Lovely", "charming", "intelligent", and "very attractive".'

'Stop it!'

At that moment Angelo returned. The women fell silent and Angelo said, 'Salvatore said he could hardly turn down a paid pub-crawl.'

'He's not seeing Muffin tonight, then?' Gina asked.

'He didn't say,' Angelo considered. 'It didn't sound as if he had to alter any arrangements.'

'Mama will be disappointed,' Gina said.

'Maybe he'll take Muffin with him,' Rosetta said. 'She certainly sounded interested when we were talking business at dinner.'

Angelo said, 'I met your friend, the salesman, today, Rose.'

'He's not my "friend",' Rosetta said.

'Forceful guy,' Angelo said.

'When I talked to him,' Rosetta said, 'he made points about the business that made sense. That's why I thought it would be good for him to talk to you.'

'What points?'

'That we should capitalize on our position in the market.'

'What does that mean?' Angelo said.

'Because Papa bought the buildings outright when he did, we have low overheads and a good location. It makes us perfectly placed to expand.'

'Do we want to expand?' Angelo asked.

'Not so far,' Rosetta conceded. 'But we have to think of the next generation. There's David and Marie. And their children. Salvatore might get married. And I haven't exactly given up the idea of having children myself yet.'


Salvatore's first stop was the Rose and Crown, a small, friendly local in Larkhall, itself virtually a village within the city. At the bar Salvatore asked for Kit Bridges' friend, Cheryl, but the man behind the bar said Cheryl wasn't on.

Salvatore ordered a pint and then bought one for the barman, whose name was Vlad. Vlad remembered the man who'd shown the photograph and described him as sallow-complexioned, and in his late twenties. As well, the man had worn a long black raincoat and was maybe five-nine. Vlad didn't remember hair colour or other features. 'Except,' he said, 'now you mention it, the bugger had knobbly hands.'

'Knobbly?' Salvatore asked.

'His fingers weren't straight. When I served him he had trouble getting a grip on the sleever, even though he'd asked for it.'

'Did he show you the picture?'

'Not *the* picture,' Vlad said. 'He had a stack of them, all the same.'

'Was he passing them out, or what?'

'Not that I saw,' Vlad said. 'But he did show one to Cheryl. I remember that.'

'And what did Cheryl tell him?'

'She asked what it were about. He said it were a hush-hush thing and he couldn't tell her details. He made it sound right mysterious.'

'But he didn't show the picture to you?'

'Not to me special,' Vlad said. 'He saw I were looking like, over Cheryl's shoulder. But he never talked to me and he never asked me direct.'

'Why not?'

'Couldn't tell you, mate,' Vlad said.

'Did you recognize the woman in the picture?'

'No,' Vlad said. 'But I wouldn't say no if Cheryl wants to introduce me.'

'I'm wondering why he showed the picture to Cheryl but not to you,' Salvatore said. 'Do you think he already knew that Cheryl was a friend?'

'Couldn't say,' Vlad said. 'Maybe he thought a girl was more likely to know another girl. Or at least more likely to admit to it.' He winked.

After Salvatore finished his drink he gave Vlad a business card and asked for a call should the knobbly-handed detective return to the Rose and Crown. Then Salvatore left and headed toward town. He stopped in several pubs along the way, but he had no joy. It was possible, of course, that the blank response he met was the same disinclination to talk to question-asking strangers that Cheryl had shown. Where they would take one, Salvatore left a card.

He made a more concerted effort at the Anchor on the edge of Kingsmead Square in town, but there too no one admitted to remembering the mysterious detective. Salvatore tried other pubs in the city centre, without success, and then he headed back toward home and the Star. At the Star he expected a more helpful reception.

And in the pokey, panelled bar he got it. Three of the men sitting at a table remembered the black-mac detective. He had been to the pub in the middle of the previous week, though there was some disagreement about whether it was on the Tuesday or the Wednesday. No one knew the man but all agreed that he had behaved in a self-important and secretive manner.

The Star, with its warren of little rooms and easy atmosphere, was the one pub in town where patrons were experienced in mixing socially with private detectives. All the adult Lunghis had drunk there over the years. 'I knew straight off he wasn't one of yours,' a Star patron told Salvatore. 'This geezer was right slimy.'

Given the sparseness of the information obtained over the earlier part of the evening Salvatore felt the 'slimy' description was worth buying his informant a pint. This largesse was rewarded because the recipient then said that, as he remembered it, the detective in the black mac had shown his picture only to women.


The Old Man had had one of his tired days. He spent the evening watching television while Mama knitted quietly across the room. One of the Old Man's favourite games was picking holes in the plots of TV mysteries. Sometimes it was just too easy and no fun, even though at other times that very ease provided the amusement. But the Old Man had other things on his mind. Namely his will. He was contemplating an alteration that would cut Salvatore out of it. He hadn't told his wife. She would be furious.

It wasn't that he *wanted* to deny his eldest child. But the boy was a wastrel. Nearly forty years old and no regular life. If he removed Salvatore from the will, and made his action public, maybe it would shock the wastrel into pulling himself together.

It was a new idea, this. The Old Man didn't quite remember when it had come to him, and it was not that he had actually done anything about it yet. His visit to the solicitor had been to explore the implications of this new plan.

But the solicitor had not proved helpful. He was only young and full of 'if that's what you want' but empty of understanding. No opinion about whether it would work, no stories of similar situations and similar experiences from other clients.

The Old Man's own solicitor – Harris, the one he'd had in mind when he made the appointment – was the man he'd dealt with ever since he started the detective business in 1947. When he couldn't join the police – an Italian so soon after the war, even though he'd spent all of it in Britain and some interned – he'd become a detective anyway. Picked Harris from a telephone directory with a pin and had been lucky. Never had a moment's complaint about Harris.

It was unfortunate for the Old Man's new intentions that Harris was dead. The Old Man now remembered going to the funeral. Five years ago? Waste of time, this youngster.

The Old Man couldn't even remember his surname. Certainly wasn't another 'Harris'. A young Harris might have been all right. But this one, no. Irritating, having to change solicitors, after all these years. In mid-stream.

But wasn't there another solicitor chap about? The Old Man couldn't remember at first. But then he did. Wasn't that chap of Rosetta's a solicitor? Seems a nice enough boy. Young, of course. Maybe not up to it himself, but he could recommend someone. Someone sensible. Someone you could talk to. What was his name, Rosetta's young man? It would come back.

'What's the name of that solicitor chap of Rosetta's?' the Old Man asked his wife.

'Walter,' Mama said without missing a knit or a purl.

Mama didn't need to ask why the Old Man wanted to know. He had spoken about enough of the pieces for her to put together the puzzle. But she did not challenge him on his ridiculous notion. She would bide her time. She would pick her moment. She said, 'How do you like this detective?'

The Old Man looked at the television screen and saw the detective, a young woman in an absurdly short skirt, show her matching knickers as she bent to get into a car. He didn't have a clue what the story was. 'Boring,' he said.


Before they went to bed Gina and Angelo talked about getting up early to follow Jack Shayler on his route to work.

'It's got to be me,' Gina said.

'Why?'

'Because tomorrow is Thursday.'

Angelo yawned. He couldn't remember the significance of Thursday. 'What am I forgetting?' he said.

'Your new computers are being delivered,' Gina said.


Mrs Shayler went to bed on Tuesday night at her normal time. But, what with all the turmoil, as she lay in bed she simply couldn't get into her book. So she waited, straining to hear the activities taking place in the rest of the house.

By the time her husband finally came to bed Mrs Shayler was reasonably sure that he had not opened the back door. And all the plumbing sounds, including the running of water in the kitchen, had occurred in their normal sequence.

However, even though Mrs Shayler had already marked the level on the Horlicks container and would therefore be able to tell in the morning whether further Horlicks had been used, she yielded to impatience. When Jack Shayler came to bed with his 'hot drink' Eileen Shayler had tried to contrive an incidental look into – or at least sniff of – her husband's mug. She had done it clumsily and he noticed.

'What are you playing at?' Jack Shayler had said.

'What do you mean?'

'Thrashing about.'

'I'm not thrashing.'

'And you never lie this close.'

'Yes, I do.'

'Not on a Tuesday you don't. Now move back to your side.'

Mrs Shayler had moved. But now she would not need to check the Horlicks box in the morning. She had established conclusively that her husband had come to bed carrying a mug of water.

Getting such dramatic information and then trying to sleep as if it were a normal night was impossible. While Mrs Shayler lay awake she could remain motionless and affect the breathing of sleep. But before dawn she finally drifted off and, thus freed, her tension and distress expressed themselves. She tossed and turned and woke her husband up.

'What's *wrong* with you?' he asked sleepily.

'Nothing,' she said. 'Go back to sleep.'

He had done exactly that. But then, in the morning, as Jack Shayler lay in bed gathering his thoughts, Eileen Shayler discovered that when her husband had retired the night before he had left his slippers in the bathroom. *And*, in depositing Tuesday's underpants in the wicker hamper, he had left them hanging on the hamper lip, *and* he hadn't put the hamper lid on properly.

Mrs Shayler could barely continue with her morning routine. It was almost an anti-climax when she found the washing-up liquid bottle standing proud on the work surface exactly where she had left it the night before.

# 6

When she arrived in the office on Thursday morning, the first thing Gina did was check her tray. In it she found Angelo's note about Charlie's phone-call saying that the police had no information about either Jack Shayler or the firm of accountants, Whitfield, Hare and O'Shea.

Once she read the note Gina did not file it. This was because in one of the many empty moments at the Crown Court the previous day she had asked the solicitors she was appearing for if they knew anything about Shayler or his employers. The response from the solicitors, too, was negative but Gina added this information to the original note and dropped it in Angelo's tray. You could never tell what detail might be important later so it was the Lunghis' policy to err on the side of thoroughness.

However, Gina mused, once the new computers were installed these memos would – or at least could – be contained inside electronic 'mail boxes'. She didn't quite know what she felt about the prospect. Might be fun, might be a nuisance. Might be both.

In her own tray Gina also found the material Adrian Boiling had left with Angelo. Gina thumbed the catalogue and leaflets. The array of gadgets was awesome, all ostensibly designed to assist surveillance work. The fun and nuisance that these implied were dark.

With the catalogue Gina found a sheet of calculations headed, 'I'll pay for myself in no time!' There was also a sheet headed, 'Have a seven-day trial, on me!'

What, indeed, had Rosetta got them into?


A few minutes past ten Salvatore arrived. 'Hello, gorgeous,' he said. 'Show us yer tits.'

Gina made tea for herself and coffee for Salvatore as he reported on his search for the slimy detective. 'There's a lot about this guy that seems odd. He's got copies of the woman's photograph, but he doesn't distribute them. And he seems to think he only needs to show her picture to other women.'

'She is a model,' Gina said. 'Models spend time with other women.'

'But why go to pubs? Why not model agencies?'

'We didn't ask this Kit Bridges if she has an agency,' Gina said. 'We spent most of the time calming her down. But maybe he doesn't know she's a model.'

'He's showing a fashion picture,' Salvatore said.

Gina wrinkled her face. 'Something's wrong about this. Something's wrong. We're missing something.'

'You want me to go and see this model?' Salvatore said. 'I could force myself.'

'Angelo's out already and he'll probably go.'

'What's he on?'

'You remember the washing-up liquid?'

'The case of the century? Of course,' Salvatore said.

'He's following the husband to work. Then he's got a bank stop but assuming the washing-up doesn't throw anything up he'll have plenty of time to see the model,' Gina said. 'Unless you *want* to see her.'

'Just trying to help,' Salvatore said easily.

'So what's with Muffin?' Gina asked.

'What about her?'

'We thought you might take her along last night. She seemed interested in the business.'

'She had something else to do.'

'What?' Gina asked.

'What do you mean, "what?",' Salvatore said.

'I thought she was here on holiday.'

'So?'

'So what else could she have to do?'


Not long after Salvatore left, the telephone rang. 'Gina Lunghi.'

'Have those computers been delivered yet?' Angelo said.

'By a sweet little old man,' Gina said. 'It only took him ten minutes to hook everything up and explain how it works. He's only just left.'

'Wives shouldn't tell lies to their husbands.'

'We'd starve if they didn't.'

'I've done the bank. I thought I'd have a word with this Kit Bridges. Has Sally been in yet?'

Gina went through what Salvatore reported.

'I agree with you,' Angelo said. 'Something's missing. I'll see what the Bridges woman has to say. Then I'll try to find her friend from the pub.'

Gina said, 'How was Jack Shayler?'

'There's something wrong there, too,' Angelo said. 'He left the house at 7.40 and he went to work. That much is like the wife said. But the route was different.'

'She said he always goes the same way.'

'Not today. From Bartlett Street he was supposed to turn at Bennett Street. But he turned at St Andrews Terrace, along the raised pavement.'

'What's there?'

'Antiques and pizza on one side. A drop to a row of garages on the other.'

'And does St Andrews Terrace lead to The Circus?'

'At the end you turn right, up a passage, and you get to The Circus by carrying on across the forecourt of the Assembly Rooms and turning left on Bennett Street. It's about the same distance. But something else happened,' Angelo said. 'In front of the Assembly Rooms.'

'Isn't that where the Costume Museum is?'

'In the basement, yes.'

'So what happened,' Gina asked. 'He tried on a dress?'

'He sat down on a bench. There's a phone box and a bench. As he walked past the phone box he looked at his watch. Then he sat down on the bench. He stayed there for two minutes. 7.49 to 7.51.'

'And?'

'He got up again and walked to his office. He went through the door there at 7.54. Apart from two minutes on the bench he didn't stop, or talk to anyone, or nod or look into a window *or* wave at a girl. He didn't pick up any packages or drop off any envelopes or shoot anybody.'

'How curious,' Gina said. 'What do you think?'

'Why tell his wife that he needs to go the same way every day but then go a different route today? What's the point of lying about things like that? It can't be important, can it?'

'You mean if a man lies to his wife it should only be about important things?'

'That's my policy,' Angelo lied.

*

46

Kit Bridges lived in a basement flat in one of the crescent terraces which ranged up the city's hillsides like an audience of toothy grins. She was home when Angelo arrived but she was about to leave. She was wearing faded denims and a black singlet and she looked stunning. Angelo was stunned.

'Are you all right?' Kit Bridges asked.

Angelo nodded. Then he said, 'We've put together a description of the detective who's looking for you.' Angelo repeated the details Salvatore had given Gina, down to the knobbly hands. 'Does it sound like anyone you know?'

'No,' Kit Bridges said. 'Cheryl described him too, but I can't think of anyone who looks like that.'

Cheryl, the friend who worked part-time behind the bar at the Rose and Crown, had a home address in the East Twerton part of the city. Kit Bridges also supplied Cheryl's phone number and the name of her own modelling agency. Then Angelo walked her to her car.

Mrs Shayler did not come to the office until just after lunch. When she arrived she went straight to a chair by the window with the plants. She looked pale and pained. She said, 'I can't go on like this. I can't. I've just painted three thatched roofs blue. It's unbearable.'

Gina made tea and even held Mrs Shayler's hand for a few minutes. Although the two women were about the same age Gina treated her client as if they were separated by a generation. Only after watching Mrs Shayler finish her tea and consume a digestive biscuit did Gina ask about events in the Shayler household the previous night.

'Everything was exactly as per normal. Not a word out of the ordinary. Not a hair out of place.'

'And did he make a drink?'

'Horlicks. For sure.'

'So whatever he's been up to didn't happen.'

'No.'

'And did you sleep?'

'Hardly a wink. Once Jack left this morning I collapsed

47

into my chair.' She demonstrated collapse in the Lunghis' chair.

'Mrs Shayler,' Gina said, 'my husband followed your husband to work today. And Mr Shayler did not take the route you gave us.' Gina described Angelo's observations, including the two-minute stop.

Mrs Shayler was devastated. 'This can't go on, Mrs Lunghi. It will kill me. This has to be resolved. It has to be resolved now.'


Angelo appeared in the office at a few minutes before four. He opened the door slowly. He saw there was no computer terminal on his desk. 'Is it safe?' he asked.

Gina, who sat at the desk, didn't say anything to her husband.

Angelo entered the room. 'Has the computer man been?'

'He's with Rosetta,' Gina said.

'Is it that Adrian chap?'

'No. Someone else. He has a moustache.'

'But he's still here.' Angelo considered. 'I want to be in position for Jack Shayler at five. I can go early.'

'No,' Gina said. There was no playfulness in her voice.

'Gina?'

'The computer man is running wires through all the walls. Your terminal will be installed tomorrow. We have other business.'

'You want a cup of tea?'

'No.'

The signs were of something serious. Angelo sat down.

'Mrs Shayler,' Gina began. 'She wants all stops pulled out. She can't bear the uncertainty. Whatever it takes.'

'So what does it take?' Angelo asked.

'She wants us to confront him. But first she wants us to put a bug in her telephone.'

'Did you ring Norse?' Norse Electronics was the company the Lunghis hired their equipment from.

'No,' Gina said.

'No?'

'For six more days we have an Adrian Boiling bug of our own. I took it out of our telephone and I set it up at Mrs Shayler's.'

'Good,' Angelo said. 'Good, good.'

'But,' Gina said, 'I put in a fresh tape.'

'We have some cassettes, don't we?'

'I found them,' Gina said. 'It's all set up at the Shaylers'.'

'So what plan did you decide?'

'Tomorrow morning follow the husband again. Then back to the house to check the tape. If something on it explains what's happening, fine. But if there isn't, we stop him on his way home from work. You decide where. Maybe at the bench.'

Angelo nodded but said, 'What do we say to him?'

'We say we've bugged his telephone. We make him ring home and get his wife to look for the bug. We pretend we're nothing to do with her.'

'Who are we to do with?'

'Anybody. We bluff, maybe make threats. Then we leave him.'

'The idea being?'

'Because it's something from the outside that he's brought into their home, Mrs Shayler can ask him what's going on.'

'Where otherwise she couldn't,' Angelo said.

'Where otherwise she couldn't,' Gina said.

'OK,' Angelo said. 'So who intercepts Shayler? Me? Sal?'

'I think both of you.'

'Good. We can work something up.' Angelo thought about it. 'By then we'll have spent most of her money. But maybe the case will be over.'

'There's something else,' Gina said.

'What?'

'When I put the bug in at Mrs Shayler's, I came back here. And there was nothing much I could do here while the computer man was back and forth everywhere.'

'So?'

'So I played the tape.'

'What tape?'

'From our telephone last night. The quality was supposed to be so good. I thought I'd check it.'

'And was it good?'

'Listen,' Gina said. There was a cassette player on the desk. She turned it on.

Angelo heard a telephone ring as heard by a caller. 'Clear,' he said.

Then the telephone was answered. A male voice said, 'Yeah?'

'Terry?' The caller was Marie.

'Who the fuck d'you think?' Terry said.

Marie said, 'I . . . I promised I'd ring tonight. Don't you remember? You said I should.'

'Did I?' Terry said. Then, 'Oh yeah. I remember something, dimly, from the smoke-filled haze hanging over the sunset.'

'What's that from?' Marie asked.

'Nothing.'

'I like it,' Marie said. 'It's pretty.'

'Pretty's no recommendation,' Terry said. 'What do you want?'

'I said I'd let you know if I was in or not.'

'In?'

'Saturday,' Marie said, losing a little patience. 'You *said* you guys needed me.'

'I don't remember "need",' Terry said.

'You said it would go better if I was there. You said we'd get more.'

'Yeah, yeah,' Terry said. 'Don't go ratty.'

'I'm not ratty,' Marie complained. 'It's just if I do it with you guys I'm going to have to lie to my parents.'

'So?'

'So nothing,' Marie said. 'It's not a problem. I lie to them all the time.'

'Well?'

'Well what?'

'Are you in or not? Because we can get someone else. *If* we decide we need somebody.'

'I'm in,' Marie said. 'I need the money.'

'Ea-sy mon-ey,' Terry sang. 'Ea-sy mon-ey.'

'Yeah,' Marie said. 'Easy money. That's what I want. They make me live on *nothing*.'

'Well, there's plenty there for the taking if we don't fuck it up. I went down and checked it out this afternoon. It's a piece of piss.'

'I looked for you in school,' Marie said.

'Schoo-ool,' Terry sang, 'ain't coo-ool.'

'This better work out,' Marie said. 'They'll kill me if they find out. I'm taking a hell of a chance.'

'Gotta gamble to win, little girl,' Terry said.

'I know,' Marie said, 'and I'm *not* a little girl.'

'Lit-tle girl,' Terry sang teasingly. 'Lit-tle vir-gin and tonic.'

'You might be surprised,' Marie said.

'Just make sure you're up to it on Saturday.'

'I'll be ready,' Marie said. 'Just make sure you guys don't chicken out or screw up.'

'You talk tough,' Terry said. 'But we'll see. Gotta go. Little girl.' He hung up.

Gina turned the tape recorder off.

Angelo didn't know what to think, what to say.

Gina said, 'Good quality recording, eh?'

# 7

Rosetta and David were late sitting down to Thursday dinner. 'Sorry!' Rosetta said as they arrived. 'We were trying the new computer.'

'It's great!' David said, eyes bright.

'Yuk,' Marie said.

'No really!' David said. 'It's not like school computers at all.'

'Yuk-a-rama, dial a llama,' Marie said.

'It's good for the boy to show enthusiasm,' the Old Man said.

'Mega-mega-mega-yuk,' Marie said, but she too appeared animated, if not about miracles of modern electronics.

Gina and Angelo both noticed Marie's alertness but they could say nothing about what most concerned them. The fault was Angelo's. He freely admitted it. He had forgotten to tell the family that their phone line was bugged on a seven-day free trial. He'd intended to say something. He never wanted to listen to their conversations. He'd only talked to this Boiling person because of Rosetta. But it was definitely Angelo's responsibility to tell everyone, and he had failed.

And violation of privacy just didn't happen in the Lunghi household. It was not talked about but it was universally understood. This was less an Italian thing than an offshoot from the fact that the family violated other people's privacy for a living. Even though this particular violation had happened innocently it couldn't possibly be admitted now.

Suddenly understanding of Mrs Shayler's inability to address her husband directly about the bottle of washing-up liquid became more complete. Families evolved their own rules, whatever they might be. What Angelo saw more clearly now was that transgression of family rules could not be undertaken, or admitted to, lightly. Rule-breaking had consequences. Rule-breaking was dangerous. A family without rules was in chaos. If Marie were to react by running away from home, no one would approve but everyone would understand.

'It might be nothing,' Angelo had said to Gina, trying to convince himself. 'He sounds like an older boy. Marie would say such things to impress him.'

But Gina was uncertain how to take what Marie had said. The tape revealed an underbelly of Marie's life that had no parallel in Gina's own teenage history. Raised in Brum, Gina had always been her family's good child, the one who studied, the one who went away to art college to do a course in textile design. For Gina, dropping out to marry a detective was the closest she'd come to rebellion. Not many girls of Marie's generation would make their break for freedom by becoming the wife of a man who was himself a dutiful son.

Finally Gina said, 'At least this Terry is still at school.'

'What do we do now?' Angelo asked. 'Set up surveillance on our own daughter?'

Gina said, 'Adrian Boiling's catalogue has a location transmitter with a Velcro strap. We can fit it around her ankle. Choice of colours.'

'Gina!'

'We wait and watch. We be patient.'

'I don't feel patient.'

'And we've got to be normal at dinner,' Gina said.

'I don't feel normal,' Angelo said. 'Suddenly I'm Papa and Salvatore's heading down a path I know is wrong.'


At dinner Mama was enlivened and distracted by the fact that Salvatore had brought Dr Muffin again. Thus the only person who might have noticed that something was up with Gina and Angelo had other things on her mind. 'It was so generous of you to bring all this wine!' Mama said.

'It's only three bottles,' Muffin said. 'And with this many people, it's really just a taste.'

'Very very generous,' Mama said. 'A lovely quality.'

'It was the least I could do, Mrs Lunghi. You're all being so kind to me. I feel almost a part of the family.' She patted Salvatore's hand.

Mama beamed. 'Call me Mama. Everybody does.'

'I don't,' the Old Man said.

'Don't mind him,' Mama said. 'He's putting the world to rights. That always makes him grumpy.'

'Huh!' the Old Man said. He was still feeling tired.

Salvatore was deputed to open the wine. Because it had come from a guest, David and Marie were each allowed half a glass.

'I'd like to propose a toast,' Muffin said. 'Is that all right?' It was. 'Here's to the Lunghi family. Beautiful people living in a beautiful city.'

Everybody drank. David said, 'Hey, this is good.'

'What would you know about it?' Marie said. She sniffed her glass. 'Though it does have a lovely bouquet.'

From his place at the head of the table Angelo began to serve the meal, vermicelli with a mushroom sauce. As the guest, Muffin was served first.

'I hope you like mushrooms, my dear,' Mama said.

'Love them,' Muffin said.

'Vermicelli,' the Old Man said.

'Wait for it,' David said.

'It means "little worms",' the Old Man said.

The children giggled. The Old Man always said that.

Muffin said, *'Vermicelli con funghi alla Lunghi?'*

'Oh yes!' Mama said. She led the family in a round of applause.

'Thank you,' Muffin said, bowing from her chair, 'thank you, friends.' Then she said, 'I've been *dying* to know something.'

'What's that, my dear?' Mama asked.

'What happened about the man with the bottle of dish-washing detergent? Is it all right for me to ask?'

'Of *course*, my dear,' Mama said.

Angelo, who had followed Jack Shayler, began to recount the developments in the case. But when Mama heard about Shayler's slippers being left in the bathroom and the used underpants being not properly put in the laundry basket, she interrupted. 'How old is this husband?'

'Forty-five, Mama,' Angelo said.

Mama nodded sagely. 'A man, when he gets older, he can't handle so much. He forgets things.'

'So you don't think the details are important?'

'Oh, they're important,' Mama said. 'It means he has other things on his mind, so he can't remember these. The wife is right to worry. This man, his slippers, it's a cry for help.'

Muffin asked, 'Did you follow him home from work too, Angelo?'

'He left work at 17.06,' Angelo said. 'And he stopped at the same bench as in the morning. He got there at 17.10, and he sat till 17.15. And what do you think he did?'

'What?' Muffin asked, but Angelo looked around the table.

'Fed the birds?' Mama suggested.

'Looked at the birds?' Salvatore said.

Angelo said, 'He checked his watch four times.'

'Wow!' Muffin said.

'What's it all about, Dad?' David asked.

'What do you think?' Angelo asked his son.

'Well,' David said, 'he might be waiting to meet someone there. Someone who walked home from school that way.'

'*School?*' Marie asked derisively. 'He's really going to be meeting someone from a school.'

'Walked home from work, I meant,' David said. 'Unless he's a perv.'

'The phone box,' Rosetta said. 'The bench is by a phone, right?'

'Right,' Angelo said. He could not prevent himself from glancing at Marie. Marie smiled.

'So it's a woman,' the Old Man said.

'But would *she* call *him*?' Rosetta asked.

'Why not?' Muffin said.

'She can't call him at home and she can't call him at work. So she calls him at the phone box.'

'Why doesn't he call her?' Rosetta asked. 'If he's already at the telephone.'

'She's sneaking around too?' Angelo said.

'He's an accountant, right, this Shayler?' the Old Man asked. Then his own question reminded him of something.

'That's right, Papa,' Gina said. 'And we don't know anything about his life other than at work and at home.'

'Hey, before I forget,' the Old Man said.

'What, Papa?' Angelo asked.

'Rosetta, that solicitor of yours.'

Rosetta flushed. The rest of the table went quiet.

The sudden stillness surprised the Old Man. He said, 'Did I get it wrong? He's a solicitor, isn't he?'

Rosetta said, 'He is a solicitor, Papa. He does conveyancing.'

'I haven't seen him lately. Where is he?'

'Away, Papa.'

'Away? Where?'

'On a trip.'

'For long?' the Old Man said.

'Yes,' Rosetta said firmly. 'For a long time.'

'Oh well,' the Old Man said. 'Can't be helped.'

Mama said, 'Have you had enough Parmesan, Muffin?'

'Yes, thank you,' Muffin said. 'Mama.'

Salvatore said, 'This telephone. Is there another phone on Shayler's route?'

Angelo considered. 'Yes, on the London Road.'

'So I say,' Salvatore said, 'he was waiting for a call. If he was making one either phone would do.'

Angelo nodded. 'Good,' he said. 'What do you think he did after he left the bench?'

'A somersault?' David said. In any case an aspirant for 'Family Wit', David was unused to wine.

'He walked to Bartlett Street, bought a bunch of yellow freesias and took them home.'

'A cry for help,' Mama said.

'Maybe even a shout,' David said.

'Sshhh,' Gina said to her son.

'Well, I think this man is totally disrupted,' Mama said. 'He tells his wife the truth about his route, but something recent changes it. This something, it's important. It upsets him. He's distracted. I think this wife is right to be worried. A good wife notices details.'

'Huh!' the Old Man said.

'Have some more wine,' Mama said. 'It's very good. You can relax. Sleep tonight.'

The Old Man held out his glass.

'May I have a little more too, please, Gran?' David asked. 'Just a little. I've done all my homework.'


After the meal Salvatore suggested that he and Muffin go to the Rose and Crown for a drink.

'Really?' Muffin said. She was obviously thrilled. 'To work on the case? Really?'

'We thought Sal might have invited you along last night,' Gina said.

'Oh, I wouldn't have been able to,' Muffin said. But she did not expand on her alternate track of holiday activities.


Vlad, the barman at the Rose and Crown, recognized Salvatore immediately. He hailed a buxom blonde woman with blue eyes and dimples who was also serving behind the bar. 'This is

Cheryl,' Vlad told Salvatore. 'Cheryl, this is the detective who was in here last night.'

'But you're not the one who came to the house this afternoon,' Cheryl said.

'That was my brother,' Salvatore said.

'Really? Is *everybody* a detective all of a sudden?'

'My brother and I are trying to find out what this other guy is up to showing pictures of your friend Kit,' Salvatore said.

'I told your brother what happened,' Cheryl said.

'Well, he said that you told him the guy in the black mac gave a copy of the picture to a woman who was in the pub that night.'

'That's right.'

'And that you said the woman is a regular?'

'Oh yeah. Bonnie's a regular.'

'Is she here?'

'No,' Cheryl said. 'But hang around. She comes in most nights before closing time.'


The subject of the slimy detective had come up toward the end of the meal. Salvatore recounted what he had found out on his pub-crawl of the night before. When he finished, the Old Man said, 'Who's paying, all this time, all these drinks?'

'We need to make sure nobody confuses this strange detective with us, Papa,' Gina said. 'And something's definitely not right about it.'

'We've got to protect the good name you built up, Papa,' Angelo said.

'Soft soap,' the Old Man said. But he was always pleased when his achievements were recognized in front of guests. 'So what's not right?'

'This detective is trying to find a woman,' Gina said.

'He should ask your brother-in-law,' the Old Man said carelessly.

Gina said, 'He has a picture, but he only shows it to women in these pubs.'

'He has copies, but he never leaves one with the bar staff,'

Angelo said. 'If he expects to find her in a pub, why not leave a copy and his phone number?'

'Except,' Gina said, 'one time he gave out a copy of the picture.'

'The barmaid friend told me this afternoon,' Angelo said. 'She saw him give one to a woman in the Rose and Crown.'

'When *we* try to find someone,' Gina said, 'we make things simple, easy for people to help us. With this man he makes everything difficult, a mystery.'

'And he has knobbly hands,' Salvatore said.

'Knobbly hands *and* a black mac,' Marie said. 'I bet he goes to pubs because he can't get anyone to go out with him. Yuk!'

'They'd have to be desperate, like you,' David said.

'You're the desperate one around here, shrimp-seed,' Marie said loftily. 'But stick with it, poor little David. Maybe one day you'll find a girl with no sense of smell who will go out with you if you *pay* her!'

'Children!' Gina said, as David was trying to frame a retort.

'But it won't be easy money for her,' Marie persisted. 'Ea-sy mon-ey!' she sang. 'Not!'

'Marie!'

'Sorry, Mum,' Marie said, without evident sorrow.

Angelo sat staring at his daughter.

'There is something wrong about this detective,' Gina said, insisting on a return to the subject. 'What he does is just not how you look for someone. Not if you know what you're doing.'

'So,' the Old Man said, 'maybe he doesn't know what he's doing. This country you can call yourself a detective, but it doesn't prove anything.'

'Is that right?' Muffin asked. 'Don't you need a licence to be a private detective here?'

'To get married, a licence,' the Old Man said. 'To fish, a licence. To drive. To fly.'

'To be an artist,' David interrupted.

'What?' the Old Man said.

'Artistic licence,' David said.

'I mean it, David,' Gina said.

'To own a big dog,' the Old Man said, 'a licence. But a private detective? Nothing!'

'Gosh,' Muffin said.

'So,' Salvatore said, 'what we've got is an incompetent detective.'

'He'd starve, the skills he shows,' the Old Man said. 'Or maybe his father owns the agency and he thinks he deserves a living no matter what. Maybe he's in for a surprise one day. Huh!'

'Finish your plate,' Mama told the Old Man. 'Gina will think you don't like it.'

'It's good, Gina,' the Old Man said, picking up his fork. 'It's good. You always make food good.'

'Thank you, Papa,' Gina said.

'Bubba,' Salvatore said, 'you saw the model today too, right?'

'Yes,' Angelo said. 'But only for a minute. She was on her way to a modelling job.'

'Bikinis?' David asked. Everybody turned to him. David hid his face.

Marie giggled. 'That's what happens when you waste good wine on *him*!'

'The model had an interview for a clothing catalogue job,' Angelo said. 'She was on her way out. But then I checked with her agency. No "detective" has asked for her there.'

'So do you think,' David said, 'that maybe this defective isn't a detective at all?'

Again everyone looked at David.

'What do you think, Sally?' Angelo asked.

'From the mouths of tipsy babes,' Salvatore said.

# 8

After dinner David and Rosetta returned to the new computer in Rosetta's office. But while it was booting up, David said, 'Auntie Rose, why isn't Walter around?'

Rosetta had consumed a good deal of Muffin's wine and was feeling no pain. She said, 'Because he's a pig.'

David didn't know whether to smile.

Rosetta warmed to the subject. 'And he's a donkey and a turd and a scorpion and a pot of goat-spray!'

David giggled. Responding to her audience's appreciation Rosetta said, 'I should have know all along he was duplicitous.'

'He was what?'

'A tricky, deceiving, grotesque imitation of a human being. It's what I should have expected from a *solicitor*.'

'A solicitor,' David repeated.

'A conniving, canoodling carpet snake of a conveyancing solicitor. But at least he's gone and good riddance!'

'Where has he gone?'

'Who knows? And who cares?' Rosetta said. 'But I'll tell you where he *should* go, where they all should go. What should happen to all conveyancing solicitors.'

'What?'

'The City Council should get a big old uncomfortable bus and they should load all the conveyancing solicitors into it and they should *convey* them somewhere. That's what they should do. They should convey them all somewhere dark and wet and radioactive. Somewhere it takes a long time to get to, because taking a long time is what they know best how to do, and even then they let you down.'

'I've got an idea!' David said. 'Let's do a computer program that gets rid of solicitors!'

'Good thinking!' Rosetta said. 'Destroy them through their modems. Spreadsheet them out of existence.' She paused. 'How?'

'There must be something we can do with the graphics,' David said.

'You want the graphics? Coming up!' Rosetta said, and they turned to the new machine.


'Do you think this Muffin is the one?' Mama said as she helped Gina load dinner dishes into the dishwasher.

'Don't get your hopes up, Mama.'

'Did you see something wrong with her?'

'A lot of Sally's women have been nice,' Gina said. 'The problem's not with them. It's him who will have to change if he's going to settle down.'

'But he would settle with the right one, don't you think?' Mama said. 'And this Muffin is not like the others. She has a thesis. And she's so interested in the work.'

Gina nodded, saying nothing.

'Is something wrong with her?' Mama asked.

Gina thought about Muffin's unknown activity the previous night. There were a hundred possibilities. Like, she went to the Theatre Royal with someone she met in her hotel. Or she met friends of her parents. Or maybe she did whatever all the other tourists who come to Bath in the summer do at night. Go to the cinema? Seek out one of those awful pizza chains Marie's friends liked so much? But why not say so?

'Gina?' Mama said.

'I don't think anything's wrong with her,' Gina said. 'She seems about perfect.'

'Me, I think so too. And she can learn to model,' Mama said. 'Now, if only I could get my Rosetta settled.'


At the dining-room table Angelo sat with Marie and the Old Man. The Old Man was dozing. Fishing for reassurance that he understood at least *something* about his daughter Angelo said, 'I'm surprised you didn't fix a day with Muffin before she left.'

'A day for what?' Marie said.

'You made a bet with her. It's not like you to forget money.'

'I didn't forget,' Marie said.

'But you know what your Uncle Sal is like with his women,' Angelo said. 'You better cash in while Muffin is still available. Unless you're afraid you won't win.'

'Of course I'm going to win,' Marie said.

'Win a bet, don't pay taxes,' the Old Man said unexpectedly. He straightened. 'How much is this bet?' he asked Angelo.

'Ten pounds, Papa,' Angelo said.

'A lot of money,' the Old Man said.

'It's not that much, Grandad,' Marie said.

'My day,' the Old Man said, 'buy a suit, get some change.'

Angelo smiled conspiratorially at Marie. He said to his father, 'You must be older than I thought if you can remember getting a suit for a tenner. Tell me, what was Queen Victoria really like?'

The Old Man made a muffled sound that could have been, 'Huh!'

Marie said, 'Nowadays ten pounds *isn't* much.'

Although he had introduced the subject, Angelo stiffened. 'Your mother negotiates your allowance.'

'I'm just saying, Daddy.'

'So what do you spend it all on?' Angelo asked. The Old Man's head dropped forward again.

'You can't even get a decent T-shirt for ten pounds,' Marie said.

'Can't you?'

'You're so out of touch with the real world.'

'Am I?' Angelo said. 'Work. Get paid for your work. Isn't that what happens any more?'

Marie's eyes narrowed. Angelo could see that she was thinking, but he didn't know about what. Had he gone too far? Did she suspect that he knew? Was that what she was working out?

'Daddy,' Marie said, 'have you got a job for me? Is that why you're talking about work and money?'

Angelo hesitated.

Marie became excited. 'Is that it? Do you? Do you, Daddy?'

'Would you be interested?'

'Of course!'

'Even though working for money's old-fashioned?' Angelo risked.

'Everybody works except Salvatore,' the Old Man said as he jerked erect again.

'Papa,' Angelo said, 'Salvatore works whenever we need him. He's out working now.'

'When it suits him,' the Old Man said. 'The family doesn't come first.'

'Daddy!' Marie said.

Angelo held up a finger. Father and daughter waited while the Old Man drifted away again.

Marie whispered, 'Don't mess about. What job?'

'Salvatore and I will talk to Mr Shayler tomorrow, right?'

'And?'

'After that we might need someone to follow him,' Angelo improvised. 'And it would have to be someone he wouldn't recognize – not me or Sal. So I thought since he doesn't have a car – as far as we know – I thought maybe you.'

'When?' Marie said. 'Tomorrow after school?'

'No, not at night,' Angelo said sternly. 'I was thinking daytime. I was thinking, Saturday.'


'What's that in your bag, Auntie Rose?' David asked.

'What?'

'It's a wine bottle!'

'No, it isn't.'

'Yes, it is! It's the one that wasn't finished.'

'Well, nobody wanted it,' Rosetta said. 'Waste is a sin.'

'Can I have some?'

'No, no,' Rosetta said. 'You had some at dinner.'

'Let me have a sip,' David said. 'Just a sip. Oh please.'

'Well . . .' Rosetta said.

'If you do I'll take the empty bottle and recycle it for you.'

'You're sure you've done all your homework?' Rosetta said, taking the bottle from her bag.

'What homework?' David said happily.

After she took a drink herself Rosetta passed the bottle to her nephew. David drank deeply.

'Enough, enough,' Rosetta said.

'Mmmmmmm,' David said. But he gave the bottle back to his aunt. 'Hey, I've thought of another one!'

'Go on.'

'Next to an ambulance station, right? Dig a deep hole. Fill it with wine. That way all the ambulance-chasing solicitors will smell the wine and fall in and drown.'

'I like it,' Rosetta said, turning to the computer and moving the cursor into the box for drawing circles. 'But instead of wine in the hole it's got to be beer.'

'Why?'

'Because that's an old-fashioned way to kill *slugs*,' Rosetta said. With her free hand she raised the wine bottle to her lips again.

'Hey,' David said. 'Hey! Leave some for me!'


Bonnie the Regular appeared in the Rose and Crown half an hour before closing time. She asked Cheryl for a pint and was surprised to find that her drink was already paid for.

'What brings this on?' she asked.

'It's not me,' Cheryl said. 'That gentleman over there.' Cheryl pointed to Salvatore who stood by the dart board. Cheryl waved to attract Salvatore's attention and Salvatore waved back.

'Him?' Bonnie said. 'But he's gorgeous!'

'Don't get excited,' Cheryl said. 'He's with the woman at the oche.'

'Probably his sister,' Bonnie said. She walked to Salvatore and touched him on the arm. 'I understand I have you to thank for my bedtime drink. What can I do in return?'

Muffin delivered a dart into the heart of the treble-twenty.


When Mama and the Old Man left to go up to their flat, Marie retreated to her room, taking the hall telephone with her. She closed the door.

On the kitchen extension Gina and Angelo saw the line-occupied light come on almost immediately. Angelo reached toward the receiver. 'I could pretend I made a mistake,' he said, but they both knew he wouldn't do it. Then they heard riotous laughter coming all the way from Rosetta's room.

When they opened the door they saw Rosetta, seated at the computer, laughing. David was on the floor, rolling and holding his sides. David said, 'Auntie Rose and I are drawing cartoons.'

Gina and Angelo moved to where they could see the computer screen.

'Run it for them,' David said.

With Rosetta at the keyboard Gina and Angelo watched as a male figure appeared on the screen. He was standing beneath a funnel. Then the image was replaced with another that had dots emerging from the funnel so it became clear that the man was standing under a shower. Next the figure was shown on its knees. Then lying flat on its face. After a moment the screen was filled with a flashing caption that read, 'Our latest legicidal spray is the most effective yet!' Rosetta and David burst again with laughter.

'What's going on?' Angelo asked.

David said, 'We're doing a series called "21st Century Ecology".'

'We're exterminating solicitors,' Rosetta said, 'to help the environment.'

'Wait! Wait! I've got a new one, Auntie Rose,' David shouted. He rolled up to a kneeling position. 'Here it is. Here it is. "One way to control the spread of solicitors is to release a zillion sterilized males.' He looked up at his aunt, expecting her approval.

But Gina and Angelo saw that Rosetta did not laugh. Her amusement turned to something else. She stiffened and turned to the screen.

'Do you get it?' David said. 'We sterilize male solicitors so they can't breed more solicitors! They did that with fruit flies in California. We studied it in school.'

Rosetta said nothing. In another moment she was fighting back tears.

'Angelo,' Gina said, 'take David to his room.'

'Is that wine I smell?' Angelo said.

'I've done all my homework!' David shouted. 'Don't you get it?'

'Rose?' Angelo said.

Gina said, 'Take David.' Angelo lifted his son off the floor by the shoulders.

'No, no!' David said. 'I've got another one. How about a solicitor swat? It's like a fly swat, only bigger.'

'Time for bed,' Gina said.

'No, no, wait!' David said, giggling, as Angelo half-carried, half-dragged him from the room.

Gina knelt on the floor next to Rosetta's chair. Rosetta was running the computer's mouse back and forth across its pad. Gina heard clicking, but didn't know what it was about. However she saw that the screen was being spoiled with a web of lines.

'Rose?' Gina said.

'He had a vasectomy,' Rosetta said.

'Walter?'

'Yes.'

'Oh,' Gina said. 'But they can be reversed sometimes.'

'Can they?' Rosetta said.

'I'm sure I've read about it.'

Rosetta turned to her sister-in-law. 'Without the man knowing?'

# 9

Angelo followed Jack Shayler to work again on Friday morning. Shayler's route, activities and timing followed exactly the Thursday morning pattern. A man of routine. Just not the particular routine he told his wife about.

When Angelo returned to the office, he and Gina shared a pot of tea and discussed how they would handle the day. Then they went to see Mrs Shayler. When Angelo and Salvatore confronted Jack Shayler later in the day and claimed they had planted a telephone bug, it would be helpful to be able to describe details of the house.

'How did Sally and I get in?' Angelo asked as they walked down the street.

'Checking for telephone faults,' Gina said.

The Shaylers' two-storey house was in a small stone terrace, one of few on the street which had not yet had its front garden paved and its honey-coloured ground floor façade knocked into a shop display window. Angelo rang the doorbell while Gina stepped across a row of pansies. From beneath the prickly leaves of a *Mahonia japonica* she retrieved a black plastic box. 'See,' she said to Angelo. 'Waterproof receiving equipment. Guaranteed.'

Mrs Shayler opened the door. The first words she said were, 'Water again last night.' She invited Gina and Angelo to come in and they did. Just inside the door a telephone rested on a small table. Next to the phone was a vase of yellow freesias.

To Gina's eye, Mrs Shayler looked better than she had the day before despite the mug of water. Perhaps it was the fact that a plan had been agreed, that she expected relief from her uncertainty and ignorance. Gina and Angelo followed their client to a small, immaculate sitting-room. Angelo studied a series of ceramic cottage scenes on the mantelpiece.

Mrs Shayler said, 'I painted those.'

'The detail is wonderful,' Angelo said.

'I use the second bedroom as a studio,' Mrs Shayler said. 'It's a north light.'

Gina opened the black plastic container. 'There was a short call. Did you use the telephone last night?'

Mrs Shayler shook her head. 'Nobody did.'

Gina played the tape and they all heard the dial tone, a number being dialled, and a telephone ringing. After ten rings the caller hung up. 'Not you?' Gina asked.

Mrs Shayler shook her head. But instead of being fearful or panicky or angry, Mrs Shayler seemed shocked.

Gina and Angelo exchanged glances. 'Do you still want us to intercept your husband on his way home from work today?' Angelo asked.

Mrs Shayler nodded.

'All right.'

Gina said, 'We'll take this tape with us. By counting the clicks we'll be able to work out the number he dialled.'

Angelo said, 'When we stop him, quoting the number will prove we've been watching him. We'll put him under as much pressure as we can.'

'Good,' Mrs Shayler said without enthusiasm.


Salvatore was in the office when Gina and Angelo returned. So too was a small man with a large moustache. Salvatore was watching the stranger attach wires to a computer terminal on Angelo's desk. The wires emerged from a fresh hole in the office wall. 'Welcome to the twentieth century, bubba,' Salvatore said.

The small man stood up. 'Mr Angelo Lunghi?' he asked brightly. 'Mrs Gina Lunghi?' He advanced on them, hand extended. 'Ignatius White,' he said. 'Adrian Boiling asked me to get these computers up and running for you. Miss Lunghi said I should take the leads through the walls.'

'Oh,' Angelo said.

'She'll soon have the business on its feet,' Ignatius White said. 'And I'll soon have your computers in working order. Will two o'clock be convenient for me to show you how everything works?'


Salvatore, Gina and Angelo retreated to the kitchen. Angelo sat with his head in his hands. 'Tea. I need tea,' he said.

Salvatore made coffee for himself and tea for the others while Gina went through the morning's events with Mrs Shayler. Salvatore said, 'We'll head for The Circus about 4.30. OK, bubba?'

Angelo said nothing.

Gina said, '4.30's good.'

Salvatore sat and reported on his meeting with Bonnie the Regular.


Bonnie had remembered the black-mac detective. 'Only too well,' she said, 'I couldn't get rid of him.'

'What do you mean?' Salvatore asked.

'He was coming on to me.'

'You really think so?' Muffin said.

Bonnie did not remove her eyes from Salvatore. 'It got to closing time and I was afraid to leave. I thought, "This guy is going to follow me home. Oh fuck!" In the end I asked Phil to scarecrow for me.'

'Phil?' Salvatore said.

'Bloke I know who was in the bar. He'll do anything for me, but I'm not interested in him, not *that* way.'

'In *The Wizard of Oz*, wasn't the scarecrow the one who wanted a brain?' Muffin said.

'But even with Phil there,' Bonnie said, 'this so-called detective nearly came out with us.'

'Are you saying you don't think he really was a detective?' Salvatore asked.

'I didn't believe a word he said. He showed me this picture, right? And I told him I'd never seen the woman. If he was the goods he'd have shoved off. That's what you'd have done, isn't it?'

'I expect so,' Salvatore said.

'But this guy starts talking about what a mystery man he is and how important the case is. It was interesting for a while, for the sheer flannel. I don't mind when someone spins me a good story, but this cloth-head couldn't even do that. In two minutes he's not looking me in the eyes, he's focusing on my boobs. Now I know they're good, but you expect a man to pretend, to be a little subtle. But this guy was drooling in my cleavage. It was obvious he wasn't looking for the woman in the picture at all. It was a pure pick-up line. Only he wasn't any good at it.'

'How would you say he rated?' Muffin asked. 'From one to ten. Or should it be from one to a hundred?'

Disdainfully, Bonnie said, 'He was just creepy. To tell the truth, he scared me.'

Salvatore said, 'Cheryl thought he gave you a copy of the woman's photograph.'

'Yeah, he did.'

'Do you still have it?'

'I chucked it this morning. I found it in my bag.'

'Did he tell you his name?'

'Oh no,' Bonnie the Regular said with a sneer. 'Not his real name. But he said I could call him Clint. Clint! Clit, more like.'

Salvatore smiled. Muffin did not. Bonnie asked Salvatore, 'Does your sister understand the joke?'

'What joke, honey?' Muffin said. 'You better explain it.'

Salvatore said, 'How about a phone number or an address?'

'He wrote a phone number on the back of the picture,' Bonnie said. 'Get a life is what I say.'

'This picture you threw away,' Salvatore said, 'might there be a way to retrieve it?'

'Well,' Bonnie said, 'I can look for it in the rubbish when I go home. But I'm not going to do it tonight. I've had a hell of a hard day. I don't intend to finish it off by rooting through orange peels and coffee grounds.'

Muffin said, 'What sort of rooting do you usually end the day with?'


Gina said, 'It sounds like your Muffin is the jealous type.'

'If they aren't before they meet me,' Salvatore said, 'they are afterwards.'

'So what about the picture?' Angelo asked.

'I'm meeting Bonnie at the Rose and Crown tonight.'

'And Muffin?' Gina asked.

'I invited her,' Salvatore said. 'But she says there's something else she's got to do.'

The telephone rang. Angelo answered it.

'Mr Lunghi!' Adrian Boiling said brightly. 'I promised I'd ring back on Friday, and I'm a man of my word. How are you liking our Telephone Interceptor? Great quality, isn't it? And one hundred per cent reliable!'


Because of routine work for other clients, it wasn't until lunch-time that Gina was able to sit down with the cassette from the Shayler bug and work out the telephone number that Jack

Shayler had dialled the night before. While she did so, Angelo made lunch.

'What do you think?' she said. 'Shall I ring it? Or do we ask Charlie to find out what it is first?'

'Ring it,' Angelo said. He rose and said, 'Shout through.' He went to the nearest extension, which was in the hall outside Marie's room.

As he waited for Gina to dial, Angelo looked at Marie's door. Impulsively he tried it. The door swung open, but when the entrance was eighteen inches wide Angelo suddenly felt resistance. Something on the floor was in the way. Angelo peered around the edge and discovered that a cardboard box was blocking the door's natural movement. The box was filled with magazines and torn wrapping paper. It blocked the door because it was wedged in place by two other boxes.

In fact, little of Marie's floor was not covered by boxes, paper flowers, sheets of notepaper, open books, cast-aside clothes, plastic wrappers, family photographs, sea shells, dead plants or cuddly toys. There was no obvious way to the bed.

Unexpectedly, Angelo found this collage of his daughter's life comforting. It was very much her own place, settled and full of things that were precious to her. Not a place she might run away from easily. He pulled the door closed again. As he did so, Gina called, 'It's ringing.' Angelo lifted the receiver.

Almost immediately the telephone was answered. 'Block Letter,' a man said.

'Who am I speaking to?' Gina asked.

'Howard,' the man said.

'May I speak to whoever is in charge, please?'

'I'm in charge now,' Howard said.

'And you're a printing firm?' Gina asked.

'That's right,' Howard said. 'What's this about?'

'What sort of printing do you undertake?'

'You name it, I can do it,' Howard said. 'If I can't do it myself, I can get it done, cheap. You won't get it for less.'

'Well,' Gina said, 'I'm ringing for Drumroll Double-Glazing.'

'Oh yeah?'

71

'We are doing a promotion in your area. In order to demonstrate the quality of our plastic glass we're replacing one window for free in selected premises.'

'For free?' Howard said.

'Absolutely free, provided the window is less than twenty-four by forty-eight inches. Free, *and* with no obligation to make other purchases. A lot of the cowboy firms have strings attached, but not us. Might you be interested?'

'I might,' Howard said. 'I got a window that size.'

'May I just confirm your address, please?'

Howard gave a street address.

'Is that in the Walcot Street area?' Gina asked.

'No,' Howard said. 'It's off the Lower Bristol Road. Do you know the railway arches?'

'Oh dear,' Gina said.

'Wrong area?' Howard said.

'I'm afraid so.'

'Never mind,' Howard said.

'You're being very understanding,' Gina said.

'I always try to be understanding,' Howard said, 'when I'm talking to a girl with as nice a voice as yours.'


'For a minute I thought we were going to have to give him a free window,' Angelo said as he spread tuna salad on a piece of bread.

'Pass the butter, will you?' Gina said. Angelo passed the butter. 'Double-glazing might be a good sideline if we've got to expand the business to cater for Rosetta's children.'


Angelo spent two afternoon hours in the office with Ignatius White. For the first hour neither the telephone nor the fax provided relief from intense computer pedagogy. White would not even break for a cup of tea. 'Tea and computers don't mix,' he told Angelo sternly. 'Spilled tea wreaks havoc with a key pad.'

When at last the telephone did ring, Angelo answered hopefully, but the caller was Adrian Boiling. 'I'm not nagging, Mr Lunghi. I don't run my business that way. I'd just like a word with my man, Mr White.' Listening to White's end of a short conversation, Angelo felt he was in a foreign country.

When the call finally finished, Ignatius White's eyes were bright and his moustache quivered. He said, 'Miss Lunghi is certainly determined to put this place to rights.'

'She is?'

'I was speaking to her earlier and she is seriously considering taking the ISDN option. I just confirmed with Mr Boiling that we can provide it.'

'You can?'

'It's a wise move, now that the telephone exchanges can handle it. ISDN makes the traditional modem obsolete, and it's more reliable and secure as well as being faster. You can send an A4 fax in two seconds, Mr Lunghi. Or the picture of a suspect, and the print is laser quality. ISDN makes sense in a business like yours. You cut your modem-related phone bills by seventy-five per cent, you use fewer couriers and it comes with installation, training, helpline and twelve months' personal support. Support,' White repeated. 'That's our middle name.'


After lunch Gina remained in the kitchen, so she heard Rosetta come up the stairs. 'I didn't know you were out,' Gina said.

'A little shopping,' Rosetta said. 'While Angelo is being trained.'

'More computers?' Gina asked.

'Not exactly,' Rosetta said. 'A skirt. A blouse.'

'Is there an occasion?' Gina asked.

Unable to contain the news, Rosetta said, 'He's asked me out!'

'Rose!' Gina said. 'When? Tonight?'

'No. Tomorrow. For lunch. And Gina,' Rosetta said, 'I think he likes me. I really think he likes me.'


Salvatore and Angelo appeared in the kitchen at about 4.15. Salvatore said, 'Gina, what's up with Rosetta?'

'What do you mean?'

'She came across to talk with the manic dwarf who was showing Angelo how to play the maracas on these new computers. Rose looked *radiant*. I've never seen her like that.'

Angelo slumped into a chair.

'Maybe you never looked,' Gina said.

'So what's up?' Salvatore said.

'Your sister,' Gina said, 'is beginning to realize she's attractive.'

'Rose?' Salvatore said. 'Attractive?'

'You're impossible,' Gina said to her brother-in-law.

'How much is being attractive going to cost us?' Angelo said tiredly.

'And *you* sound just like your father,' Gina said.


The Old Man sat at his desk. He held a folder of documents but he wasn't reading them. From their little kitchen Mama brought him out a cup of tea. She set it by the documents. 'You ready for this?' she asked.

'Ah,' he said.

'Are you all right?'

'What else?' the Old Man said. He did not turn around.

Mama bent over the back of her husband's chair and put her arms around his shoulders.

At first the Old Man shrugged the touch off, not recognizing it as affection. Then he accepted the gesture.

When Mama stood straight again the Old Man said, 'What brought that on?'

'Just thinking,' Mama said. 'Just thinking what a lovely, lovely family we have.'

The Old Man nodded.

'All of them,' Mama said.


'I told my parents I'll be with you tomorrow,' Marie said as she waited with Jenny at the bus stop after school.

'So you're going to do it, Marie?' Jenny said.

'Terry's counting on me now,' Marie said coolly. 'I don't want to let him down. You know what men are like when you disappoint them.'

'Ooo, you're so *brave!*'

'Money's money,' Marie said, 'no matter how you get it.'

'But if you get caught . . .' Jenny persisted. 'If your parents find out . . .'

'I'll just run away with Terry,' Marie said. 'I'm sure he'd do the honourable thing.'

'That's not what Olive says,' Jenny said.

'Olive,' Marie said. 'Huh!'

'My mum would roast me,' Jenny said. 'And my *dad*! He'd probably explode with flashing lights like one of the monsters in Hector's games.'

'I think we're a little more mature than that in our household,' Marie said.

'But,' Jenny said, 'if you do get caught . . .?'

'You keep talking about getting caught. Why don't you ask what I'm going to do with all that beautiful money?'

'What?'

'I don't *know*!' Marie said in peals of giggles. 'We can decide tomorrow night.'

'*Great!*'

'Where shall we go?'

'Olive thinks they're cracking down on IDs at the Cat and Fountain,' Jenny said. 'Her sister says the police came in the other night.'

'That's good,' Marie said.

'Is it?'

'If the police are worrying about under-age drinking, it'll keep their minds off *other* things.'

'*Oooo!*' Jenny said.


Angelo and Salvatore stood waiting beneath the plane trees which canopied the middle of The Circus.

'Papa says The Circus was modelled on the Colosseum in Rome,' Angelo said. 'Is that right?'

Salvatore smiled. 'Papa also says the carvings along the roofline are pineapples.'

'Aren't they?'

'Acorns,' Salvatore said.

'Those are acorns?'

'They have to do with the legend of leprous Prince Bladud and his pigs. His pigs liked acorns.'

Angelo looked at the acorns again. Then he looked at his watch. 'Nearly time.' He counted to seven. 'Now.'

Both men looked to the door of Whitfield, Hare and O'Shea. It opened.

'Huh!' Angelo said.

A woman emerged. She looked at the sky, and then closed the door behind her.

Salvatore said, 'Is that him, bubba?'

'Surveillance has never been an exact science,' Angelo said.

Fifty seconds later Jack Shayler left his office.


As they followed Shayler across the open space in front of the Assembly Rooms, Angelo said, 'I want to see if he stops at the bench. If he does, we'll do him there. If not, in the passage.'

As Shayler approached the bench by the telephone at the end of Alfred Street he looked at his watch. He sat down.

Within seconds Angelo and Salvatore sat either side of him. Shayler looked from one to the other. He was a pallid man with sandy hair that seemed a dusty outline to his face. He was clearly surprised by the imposing company. 'We've been looking for you, Jack,' Angelo said.

'How do you . . .?'

'You've been making telephone calls, Jack,' Salvatore said. He reeled off the number that Shayler had dialled the previous night.

'Sound familiar?' Angelo said. 'Bit naughty, making secret phone calls before you go to bed.'

Shayler's jaw flopped down and hung open.

'I expect you want to know how we know,' Salvatore said. 'Well, we've been in your house.'

'Nice freesias by the phone,' Angelo said.

'Yellow,' Salvatore said. 'My favourite.'

'And while we were admiring them, we left a little ear in the telephone,' Angelo said.

'That's right,' Salvatore said. 'We bugged your telephone, Jack.'

'But you'll want to confirm that, I expect,' Angelo said.

'I've got an idea,' Salvatore said. 'Why don't you ring home, Jack? Ring your wife.'

'Nice woman, your wife,' Angelo said. 'Trusting. Open. Pity if something happened to a nice woman like that.'

'You ring her,' Salvatore said. 'Make sure she's all right. And then tell her to unscrew the part of the phone she talks into.'

'It comes off easy,' Angelo said.

'And tell her to look for a little brown cube.'

'Smaller than a sugar lump,' Angelo said.

'Oh yes, much smaller,' Salvatore said. 'But it's a modern miracle, Jack. It is, because it picks up telephone conversations a treat.'

'So let's do that before we go any further, Jack,' Angelo said. 'You check our bona fides with your wife. And then, Jack, then we'll have a little talk about what you're up to, eh?'

'What's the matter, Jack? Cat got your tongue?'

At long last Jack Shayler said, 'Who . . . who are you?'

'First things first, Jack,' Salvatore said. 'Ring the missus.'

'I don't . . .' Shayler said.

Angelo and Salvatore each took an arm. They lifted Shayler to his feet and manoeuvred him to the red telephone box. Angelo went in first. The idea was that Salvatore would wedge Shayler in from behind while Angelo dialled the Shaylers' home number. Angelo had a coin ready.

But with unexpected strength Jack Shayler suddenly twisted out of Salvatore's grip and bolted down Alfred Street.

Angelo stepped out of the telephone box and stood with his brother as they watched Shayler sprint away. 'Quick for an accountant, isn't he?' Angelo said.

'Caught me by surprise, bubba,' Salvatore said. 'Sorry.'

'Should be all right,' Angelo said. 'He'll arrive home out of breath. His wife can ask him about that.'

'Should we follow him, do you think?' Salvatore asked.

'Yeah,' Angelo said. 'To make sure he doesn't stop to rest. But first I'll ring his wife to tell her what happened.'

But as Angelo turned back to the phone, it rang.


# 10


Dinner on Fridays was always early and cold. The pattern first evolved at the height of the Norman Stiles case, the Old Man's only murder. The subjects of the Stiles surveillance pursued their nefarious activities during active weekends that began on Friday evening. Because the Stiles case was complicated and lengthy, a Friday and Saturday routine of simple meals was established.

The pattern still suited the Lunghis because it allowed those with social and cultural inclinations to go out early. Salvatore, the Marie of his day, always had 'plans' but in those days everyone in the family went out occasionally. More recently it was the newest generation of Lunghis who most often socialized on Friday and Saturday nights. And, until the last few weeks, alternate Fridays were when Rosetta regularly got some time alone with Walter.

This Friday, however, was almost unprecedented. Everyone was at dinner – even Salvatore – and no one was in a hurry. When Mama and the Old Man came down from their flat and saw how full and settled the household was they were both surprised.

The Old Man was pleased. 'The washing-up liquid, it pulls them in,' he said.

Mama's feelings were more ambivalent. She said to Salvatore, 'You're going out later?'

'Yes, Mama. To the Rose and Crown to pick up the picture

the so-called detective left with the woman Muffin and I talked to last night.'

'And Muffin? How is she?'

'Fine,' Salvatore said.

'She's going with you?'

'Not tonight.'

Mama would have said more but the Old Man said, 'You met this Shayler husband today, yes?'

Salvatore said, 'That's right, Papa. On his way home from work.'

'And you put the wind up him?'

'We filled his sails,' Salvatore said. He smiled at his brother.

Angelo said, 'Good and proper, Papa.'

'Did he admit the fancy woman?'

'It's more complicated than that, Papa,' Angelo said.

'Life is complicated,' the Old Man said. 'So?'

Angelo began by recounting the visit he and Gina made to Mrs Shayler in the morning, and how it had produced the telephone number Jack Shayler tried the previous night. Gina went through the phone conversation the number had produced with Howard the Printer in the early afternoon. Then Salvatore and Angelo described the late afternoon encounter with Jack Shayler.

'And the public phone ringing was no wrong number?' the Old Man asked.

'It was Howard,' Angelo said.

'Howard?' the Old Man said. 'The printer?'

'That's right, Papa,' Angelo said.

'Wow!' David said. 'It all fits.'

'Huh!' the Old Man said. 'So it's not a woman with Shayler after all.'

'It was definitely Howard,' Angelo said. 'I recognized his voice.'

'So what is it between Shayler and this Howard? He's a boyfriend maybe?'

'I think not,' Angelo said. 'Howard was angry and he was shouting.'

Salvatore said, 'I could hear him and I wasn't even on the phone.'

'And this angry printer, what did he say?' the Old Man asked.

'He said, "All right, I rang. You happy? But I'm not talking to you. My job is my business, right? And nothing to do with you. So if you know what's good for you you'll keep your fucking nose out of it." Then he hung up.'

'"If you know what's good for you",' the Old Man said. 'Angry.'

'What's it about, Dad?' David asked.

Angelo repeated what he had heard Howard say and then asked everyone, 'What do you think?'

Salvatore said, 'I think Shayler initiated contact and has been pushing Howard to ring back, something to do with his job.'

'And Howard doesn't want to talk about it,' Gina said. 'In fact he threatens.'

'But Shayler doesn't know that,' Salvatore said, 'because he never got the call.'

'But he probably thinks you and Angelo came from Howard,' Gina said, 'so he didn't get the call but he got the message.'

'What's so difficult for this Howard about talking?' Mama said. 'Anybody can talk. What does it cost?'

'Maybe it's something they shouldn't talk about,' Rosetta said.

'Or something Howard keeps secret and Shayler shouldn't know about,' Angelo said.

'Porn?' David suggested. He was rewarded for his suggestion by a sharp look from his mother. 'I was just trying to think of something to do with a printer,' David said.

'Don't forget the cry for help,' Mama said. 'This Shayler is upset, disturbed. Whatever it is.'

'Maybe Mr Shayler is trying to blackmail the printer,' David said.

'Could be,' Angelo said. 'But blackmail about what?'

Marie stood up. 'You shouldn't say "blackmail",' she said.

'I think it could be blackmail,' Angelo said. 'It would explain why Howard is so angry.'

'You shouldn't say the word, "blackmail". It demeans black people to associate them with bad things all the time.'

Marie's declaration stopped other conversation.

'What? What did she say?' the Old Man asked Mama.

Marie said, 'I've got some calls I have to make.' She left the room.

'Well well,' Mama said. 'Is it, maybe, love?'

'I think it's a cry for help,' David said.

Gina said, 'Does she have a new boyfriend, David? Do you know anything?'

'No, Mum.'

'But you see her around school.'

'Only with her boring, stupid girlfriends.'

'What I don't understand,' the Old Man said, 'is how Shayler connects with a printer.'

'We were talking about Marie,' Mama said.

'Marie?' the Old Man said. 'We were talking about angry Howard, the printer.'

'I don't think there's anything more to say about Marie, Mama,' Gina said.

'Is something wrong with Marie?' the Old Man asked. He looked around the table. 'Is she sick?'

'Lovesick,' David said. Then he held up his hands. 'Only kidding, Mum, only kidding.'

'She's lovesick?' the Old Man said. 'Huh. She'll get over it.'

'What were you saying, Papa?' Angelo asked.

'Girls get lovesick,' the Old Man said. 'Then one day they feel better. It's like it never happened. Who can understand? It happened with Rosetta.'

'Papa!' Rosetta said.

'Always mooning after someone,' the Old Man said. 'I noticed. I knew.'

'Tell about the printer,' Mama said.

'What about the printer?' the Old Man said. 'I don't know about the printer. Except he's angry. Also I don't know how the printer knows Shayler. How they connect.'

'Good question, Papa,' Angelo said.

Salvatore said, 'Surely, the connection must come through Shayler's job. Maybe Shayler's firm does the accounts.'

'Is Howard's business a big one?' Rosetta asked.

'I doubt it,' Gina said. 'He answered the phone himself and spoke as if he could make decisions.'

'If it's small he wouldn't have expensive accountants.'

'They're expensive?' the Old Man asked.

'Their office is in The Circus, Papa,' Rosetta said. 'They're not going to be cheap. They must have high overheads.'

'And all the latest equipment,' Angelo said quietly.

'Time to take a look at this printer,' the Old Man said. 'If someone is paying.'

'Mrs Shayler's still paying,' Gina said.

'Poor woman,' Mama said. 'What she must be going through.'

'I rang her from the pay phone,' Angelo said. 'But I didn't talk to her for long.'

'She needed to be ready for her husband running home,' Gina said. 'Ready to ask why he was so upset.'

'And sweaty,' Salvatore said.

'After the call we followed where Shayler ran but we couldn't see him anywhere,' Angelo said.

'So we have to assume he went straight home,' Gina said.

'Back to the nest,' Mama said.

Gina said, 'I wish we could ring Mrs Shayler now, to ask what happened.'

'And make sure he did go home,' Angelo said.

'Where else?' Mama asked. 'A disturbed man. Frightened by bullies. Of course he runs to his wife. He's lucky he has a wife. Single men aren't so lucky.' She looked at Salvatore.

Gina said, 'But since we can't ring her, we'll have to wait for her to contact us.'

'Time to look at this printer,' the Old Man said again.

'Angelo and I thought we'd go over there this evening,' Gina said. 'There's an address off the Lower Bristol Road.'

'Good,' the Old Man said, nodding. 'Good. This salad dressing, it's that low cholesterol muck?'

'Of course not,' Mama said. She winked at Gina.

'Tastes it,' the Old Man said.

'Do you want me to get you some extra cholesterols from the kitchen, sprinkle them on?' Mama said. 'Because I can't. But taste the fresh basil.'

'I just asked,' the Old Man said.

As the Old Man spooned salad dressing on to his tomato slices David said, 'Auntie Rose, can we work with your new computer tonight?'

'Don't push your luck,' Angelo said.

'I want to work on our cartoons,' David said. 'That's all right, isn't it? I don't have any homework this weekend.'

'What pushing your luck?' the Old Man said. 'Is there pushing luck on a computer? Like a button? Rosetta?'

But Rosetta said, 'I won't have time, tonight, David. You can use the computer but it will have to be on the office terminal, not mine.'

'Dad?' David said. Angelo said nothing. 'Mum?'

'Yes, all right,' Gina said. 'If you're not going out.'

'Are you going out tonight, Rosetta?' Mama said.

'No, Mama.'

'So why so busy you can't help David learn?'

'Didn't Gina tell you? I've got a lunch date tomorrow.'

'Have you!' Mama said.

'So I've got to wash my hair and decide what to wear and try to relax.'

'Who's it with, Rose?' Angelo asked.

'Don't bully the poor girl,' Gina said. 'It's not your business.'

'I wasn't bullying.'

Mama said, 'Must be important if you need to relax tonight.'

'Mama!' Rose said.

'I'm not prying,' Mama said. 'I wouldn't pry. All I hope is this one isn't married.'

Rosetta said nothing.

'Is he married, Rose?' Gina asked.

'I . . . don't know,' Rosetta said.


The Lunghis' garage was not behind the house but a path at the foot of the garden led, circuitously, to the road the garage was in. After loading the dishwasher Gina and Angelo headed down the path on the way to their car and their trip to the Block Letter premises of Angry Howard the Printer.

The path was tree-lined and overlooked the Avon. As if by prearrangement they stopped at the riverside and Angelo took Gina's arm. A tourist launch passed on its way back to the centre of the city and a cluster of children waved from it. Gina and Angelo waved back. As the launch's wake approached, Gina felt a wave of relaxed satisfaction.

The river and the hills on either side, piled with their terraces like cornflakes in a bowl, had contributed to the eighteen-year-old Gina's choice of Bath over the other art colleges when she was picking her textile course. Of course it was a long time ago now. Many an Avon gallon had passed under Cleveland Bridge.

Gina had been in the city for only two weeks – already, embarrassingly, homesick for the family she'd won the right to a career from – when a devastatingly handsome third-year picked her out. 'Do you realize what a beautiful couple we'd make?' he'd said, his first words. Gina realized nothing of the kind, but was pleased at the attention and enjoyed his bright energy. Remarkably, for their first date he invited her home.

Gina wondered if Mama ever wished it had been Salvatore she'd married. Whether Mama thought she would have been 'the one' to steady him down. But from the beginning Gina found Salvatore as disturbing as he was attractive. Beautiful, and attentive, but fundamentally unsafe. However she had *loved* the family and, soon, the younger brother who was already a mainstay in the family business.

'So what about Marie?' Angelo asked.

'What about Marie?'

'Do we do anything?'

'What did you have it in mind to do?' Gina asked.

'I don't know,' Angelo said. 'Yes, all right, do we try to find out what she's up to? What would we recommend to a client?'

Poor Angelo. So upset by all this, because he couldn't *understand* it. 'Who's paying?' Gina said.

But Angelo did not wish to be deflected. 'Is it not important?' he asked. 'To me it sounded important.'

'Children lie to their parents,' Gina said. 'And if they don't, they lie to their friends and say they do.'

'But "easy money"?' Angelo said. 'What's that supposed to mean? What money is easy?'

'I don't know,' Gina said. Marie was growing up in a different world from the one Gina grew up in. 'Maybe it's a job of some kind.'

'I offered her a job,' Angelo said.

'You did?'

'For this Saturday. She turned it down.'

'She's already committed,' Gina said. 'And it could be paying work.'

'If it was a legitimate job, she would brag,' Angelo said. 'To annoy David.'

'I believe she's fundamentally sensible,' Gina said. 'Don't you believe that?'

'Is she? Pop concerts too young. Night-clubs with bands. Expensive tastes . . .'

'You're working yourself up,' Gina said. 'What do you want to do?'

'I just think we ought to consider what we would do for a client. If we give good advice, shouldn't we take some of it ourselves?'

'Follow her?'

'Maybe it's necessary. Maybe it's important. Maybe we should.'

'I don't want to start following our own children,' Gina said.

'I don't *want* to either, but what if it's a robbery?' Angelo said. 'This Terry had been to check the place out. Is he casing the joint? Or maybe it's shop-lifting. A lot of them do that, don't they? "Easy money," she said. At table she even sings it.'

'You think Marie is stealing? You might as well say she's selling drugs. Or her body.'

'Don't forget the infatuation,' Angelo said. 'You heard the tape. It was in her voice. They can go crazy for love, girls. Look at Rosetta.'

\*

85

When Salvatore arrived in the Rose and Crown Bonnie the Regular was already there. 'I was beginning to think you didn't really want this phone number,' she said.

'Oh, but I do,' Salvatore said. His smile, his teeth, his eyes all said he wanted it.

'So, you going to get me a drink, or what?'

Salvatore bought drinks for them both.

'Cheers,' Bonnie said. 'Where's your sister tonight?'

'Washing her hair,' Salvatore said before he caught up with the fact that Bonnie was asking about Muffin, not Rosetta.

'She's not your type, you know,' Bonnie said.

'You don't think so?'

'Too nervy. The nervy kind wears thin after a while, don't you think?'

'You could be right,' Salvatore said.

'Bottoms up,' Bonnie said, raising her glass.

'*Salute*,' Salvatore said. They both drank deeply.

'I didn't bring the picture with me,' Bonnie said.

'That's not very helpful of you.'

'Thing was, I found it in the rubbish, under coffee grounds and wet lettuce trimmings. I was in muck up to my elbow.'

'I'm very grateful,' Salvatore said.

'I had to have a long, hot, steamy bath to clean up after I pulled it out.'

'But you did find it?'

'I did. And I wiped all the gunk off and hung it on my clothesline to dry. But when I came out, I forgot it.'

'And was the number he wrote on the back legible?'

'Oh, I think so.'

'You didn't happen to write it down?'

'No. Sorry.'

'Or memorize it?'

Bonnie concentrated. 'Four, six . . . No, I don't remember. Sorry.'

'But it was a Bath number?'

'Yes. I prefer a bath number to a shower number, don't you?'

'There's a place for verticality as well as horizontality in a full, rich life, don't you think?' Salvatore said.

'*Touché,*' Bonnie said.

'So,' Salvatore said, 'what are we going to do about this?'

'You really want this telephone number?' Bonnie said.

'I do,' Salvatore said.

'Well, I suppose when we finish our drinks we'll have to go back to my place for it.'

# 11

Gina and Angelo had difficulty locating Block Letter. The road Howard had named was on the map, but it barely warranted the notoriety. It was a narrow pot-holed lane and it ran along the base of the railway bridge which supported the main line track on its way out of Bath to Bristol. The bridge arches had been filled to make workshops, their fronts looking like a row of tombstones. Block Letter was one of them, but it was identified only by a carelessly hand-painted sign that hung unevenly above the door in its wooden front. Next to the door, barely two feet square, a window gap had been cut. It was covered by chicken wire on the outside and a piece of patterned plastic inside. 'Hardly worth the bother of double-glazing it,' Angelo said.

There was no sign of life inside Block Letter. Even so, Angelo tried the door. It was locked but it rattled and did not seem particularly secure.

'Shall we?' Gina said.

'If we break in, what are we looking for?' Angelo said. He rattled the door a few more times, then left it.

Gina said, 'I can't imagine a business in Bath less likely to have its accounts done by a firm in The Circus than this one.'

'A busker?' Angelo said, but he was accepting her point.

Gina stepped back from Block Letter and then began to walk along the row of arched workshops. Angelo looked in the other direction. Of the three premises two were unidentified – perhaps storage units – and the third offered to repair 'white household appliances'. A matter for the Commission on Racial Equality? Cause for concern on behalf of otherly-coloured domestic machines? 'Blackmail', huh! He turned and followed Gina.

Ahead he saw her knock on a door. She called, 'Hello? May I come in?' Though Angelo could hear no response, Gina disappeared inside.

Before he got to the doorway Angelo could smell paint and solvent and he recognized the business as a car body shop. As he entered, Gina said, 'And this is my husband.'

A figure in splotched canvas overalls put down a spray nozzle. The figure unfolded itself from behind a yellow Fiesta. As it lifted a hood with goggles from its head, the figure became a woman with a quantity of light brown hair bulging through a hairnet. The woman said, 'How do?'

Gina said, 'We're looking for Howard. Do you know him? The man in Block Letter, the printing place down the road?'

'Wouldn't expect him to be there this time of night,' the woman said. 'Or were he supposed to meet you?'

'We thought he might be in,' Gina said.

'Pretty much keeps to business hours now he's got the place to hisself,' the woman said.

'So, it's just him who works there?' Gina asked.

'Drives a red Jag,' the woman said.

'A Jag?' Angelo said.

'I sorted it out for him. A '78 and it needed a lot doing. I only finished about a month past.'

'I wouldn't mind driving a Jag, even a '78,' Angelo said.

'It's a nice motor now,' the woman said. 'I did a good job, if I do say so meself. Body's nigh perfect. I put in an automatic gearbox. And I customized the interior, for socializing, shall we say.' She grinned. 'All the girls'll go for a motor like that, I shouldn't wonder.'

'Block Letter is doing pretty well, then, is it?' Angelo asked.

'I'd say more steady than well. But he's fell on his feet, has

Howard. He's only been in charge for the five month. He were some sort of apprentice afore that, but the old fella that took him on up and died. Howard thought he was back on the dole for sure but then the owner said he'd give Howard a try and it seems to be working out.'

'So the actual owner doesn't work there?' Gina said.

'No, no. Couldn't tell you where he does work, mind, but he needs a lot of printing so I guess he reckoned it was more economic to set someone up. Reg Adamson, the old fella that died, he were redundant a few years back so I daresay he worked cheap.'

'He didn't drive a Jag, then?' Angelo said.

'No,' the woman said with a smile, 'but he did have a soft spot for old guns, antique weapons, like. Made a few bob repairing and restoring before he took up the printing again. Nice old codger, he were. Always said "How do?"'

'Do you know how long Block Letter's been there?' Gina said.

'Not as long as me. 'Bout three and a half years, I'd say.'

'So a fair while,' Gina said.

'Do you know the owner's name, by any chance?' Angelo asked.

'No. Sorry.' The woman looked from Angelo to Gina. 'What is it you want there?'

'Some advertising flyers,' Gina said.

'Old Adamson, he printed nothing but what he printed for the owner. Howard's spread his wings a bit. He's got him a lifestyle in mind that he'd like to have to support. It's only an old press in there, but if what you want him to print ain't too fancy he should be able to handle it.'

'Do you know Howard well?' Gina said.

'Nothing personal,' the woman said. 'I go for a bloke with a bit more meat on him, meself, not that I spurn the gristle. But Howard stopped by most every day to see his car while I were working on it. So I got to know him.'

'And what's he like?' Gina asked.

'A lot of folks would find him an odd one, but the fella don't bother me. Bit twitchy, maybe. Quiet when you expect him to talk, talky when you expect him to be quiet, you know? But he's got plans. And he's trying to make the best of his luck, you can tell that.'

'Mine, all mine,' Bonnie the Regular said as she unlocked the door to a small terraced house five minutes' walk from the Rose and Crown. 'You like?'

'Very nice,' Salvatore said as he was led inside.

'Make yourself comfortable,' Bonnie said. She gestured to a futon that was rolled up into a couch. Salvatore sat. 'Let me get you a drink. How about some wine? Would you like a little white wine?'

'Great,' Salvatore said. 'But – '

'But you want the picture,' Bonnie said. 'That doesn't mean I have to keep you on the doorstep, does it?'

'Thank you.'

'Fancy something to eat? I could put together a sandwich, no trouble.'

'Just the wine, thanks,' Salvatore said.

'Or toasted cheese? I do a mean toasted cheese. It's one of my main culinary accomplishments. In a kitchen, anyway.'

'Well, as a matter of fact I haven't had anything cooked tonight,' Salvatore said.

'Your sister doesn't run to anything hot?' Bonnie asked.

Despite the allure of the new equipment, David found that drawing cartoons on a computer screen was time-consuming and frustrating. After a while he decided to make rough sketches first, using technology dating from an earlier era: pencil and paper.

These were so user-friendly that when the telephone rang it was several rings before he reacted. But eventually he put down his pencil, leaned back in his father's chair and took the receiver off the hook. 'Lunghi Investigation Services. David Lunghi speaking.'

'Davey?' Muffin said.

'Muffin?' David said. 'Or should I call you Dr Muffin?'

'Y'all can call me whatever you like, honey,' Muffin said.

'Uncle Sal isn't here,' David said. 'Not unless he's over in the house. I'm in the office. I've got a little work I'm trying to get done.'

'You poor thing. I guess they must work you to the bone,' Muffin said.

'Not really,' David said, both pleased and embarrassed that Muffin had responded to the hint that he was working on one of the family's cases.

'But it wasn't Salvatore I wanted to talk to,' Muffin said.

'It wasn't?' David said. He heard a motor vehicle pass in the background where Muffin was calling from.

Muffin said, 'Is your mom there, honey?'

'I'm afraid not,' David said.

'Damn,' Muffin said with surprising force.

Having registered that Muffin was ringing from a pay phone, David began to recognize that for Muffin to do so in order to speak to Gina was unusual. But he couldn't think of what to say to help or make Muffin feel better. He said, 'Mum and Dad are both out.'

'It was your mom I wanted,' Muffin said quietly.

There was a silence. David felt that he was expected to fill it. 'That's why I'm covering the phone in the office,' he said. 'But I'm also working on the new computer. You were right. It's great. What I've been doing is some cartoons, actually. Last night I thought them up. Well, Auntie Rose and I did. But I'm working on them alone tonight.'

'That sounds fine, honey. But can you tell me when your mom is going to be back? Do you know?'

'I don't, but I can leave her a message. She could call you back as soon as she gets home.'

'I don't know if I'm going to get back to the hotel tonight. I guess I'll just have to try to catch up with her tomorrow.'

'OK,' David said. Muffin hesitated without hanging up. David said, 'Muffin?'

'Just thinking if there's anything the hell else I can do, honey. But there isn't.' Then she hung up without saying goodbye.

As David hunted for a message card, he was in a state of considerable agitation. Muffin was upset about something, maybe even in trouble. He should have offered help. Offered Charlie's number if she needed the police. Or offered to come out to wherever she was. But instead he'd rabbited on about his cartoons. Why was he so stupid! David pounded the desk half a dozen times. One of his pencils rolled on to the floor.

He found a message card and headed it, 'Gina'. He recorded Muffin's name and the time. 'No message,' he wrote, 'but she said she'd try to catch up with you tomorrow.'

Thinking about the rest of what Muffin had said, David fixed on the phrase, 'I don't know if I'm going to get back to the hotel tonight.' It struck him as slightly titillating. And combined with 'Just thinking if there's anything the hell else I can do,' it definitely suggested a problem.

David leaned back. He *should* have offered to come out and help her. 'Is there anything *I* can do?' he should have said. To have been able to leave a note that said, 'I am out helping Muffin,' would have been very pleasing.

David rocked forward again and decided to add to his message, 'I don't know whether it matters but she was ringing from a pay phone, it was you she asked for, not Uncle Sal, and she said she didn't know if she was going to get back to her hotel tonight.' He studied the card as written. He initialled the card 'D.L.' and returned to his cartoons.

Almost immediately the telephone rang again. 'Muffin?' he said.

There was a pause at the other end of the line. Then a woman whispered, 'Mr Lunghi?'

David realized he had made a mistake, that it was not Muffin. He said, 'Yes. David Lunghi.'

'Eileen Shayler here. It's my husband. He's panicking. He thinks the two of you tried to kill him. You didn't, did you? No, of course you didn't. But he doesn't know *what* to do. I think maybe you'd better think of some reason to come round here in the morning. I don't know what reason, but . . .' The woman hung up.

David held the telephone receiver in his hand while he absorbed what had happened. Mrs Shayler! Quickly, he wrote another message card and did his best to reproduce what Mrs Shayler had said, word for word. Then he sat back and tried to think of something he could *do*.

'This *is* good,' Salvatore said with genuine enthusiasm.

'A bit of mustard is the secret,' Bonnie said. 'And I grind my own sea salt.'

'It goes very well with the wine,' Salvatore said. 'A guy could feel spoiled here.'

'Could he?'

'You know, Bonnie,' Salvatore said, 'you have very good bone structure.'

'Oh yeah?'

'I mean it. Have you ever modelled? Seriously?'

'Seriously?' Bonnie said. 'No. I've never modelled. Most of the men I meet seem to think it's their own bone structure that's good.'

'Because I'm a painter,' Salvatore said.

'I thought you were a private detective.'

'Only when my brother wants some help. My real line is painting.'

'Your real chat-up line?'

'Seriously,' Salvatore said. 'I'm serious.'

'Well, I don't feel very serious,' Bonnie said.

'Maybe we can be serious later,' Salvatore said.

'Later,' Bonnie said. 'That sounds promising.'

Salvatore rose with his plate. 'Can I wash this up?'

'House-trained too? Be still my beating heart.'

'It seems only fair since you cooked for me.'

'I thought maybe it was time to take a look at this picture you're so hot for?'

Salvatore put the plate on a table. 'Where is it?'

'On my clothes-line. Which just happens to be in my bedroom.'

'I think it's essential that I see the picture without further delay,' Salvatore said.

Bonnie rose from the futon, then held out her hand. Salvatore took it and as he did Bonnie leaned forward so that their lips brushed. Then Bonnie wheeled and pulled Salvatore toward the stairs. The resistance she met was not great.


'We need to take a look at this Howard,' Angelo said as he and Gina sat in their car. 'Pity it's the weekend.'

'Maybe tomorrow morning,' Gina said. 'Places can be open on Saturday morning.'

'If he isn't too tired after driving girls around in his Jag,' Angelo said.

'Is that what you'd do if you had a Jag?'

'Certainly not.'

'What then?'

'I'd drive women,' Angelo said.


Somewhat to Salvatore's surprise, in Bonnie's bedroom there actually was a clothes-line with a photograph hanging from it, held by two pegs. 'There 'e be,' Bonnie said. 'The famous picture.'

Salvatore took the photograph down. He looked first at the picture of Kit Bridges. Bonnie stood by his side. 'What about her bone structure?' she said.

'It's excellent,' Salvatore said with the cruel dispassion of the artistic eye. He turned the photograph over. The word 'Clint' was printed in large letters with the telephone number below it. The number was slightly smudged. Salvatore took it closer to the light.

'One telephone number,' Bonnie said. 'I always try to deliver what I promise.'

But Salvatore did not speak as he studied the telephone number.

'Mr Detective?' Bonnie said.

Finally Salvatore looked up. 'I don't know how to say this,' he said.

'What?'

'I'm going to have to leave now.'


Marie knocked gently on Rosetta's door. 'Auntie Rose? Are you awake?'

From inside Rosetta called, 'Marie?'

'Can I come in?'

'Of course.'

Marie opened the door and went in. Rosetta sat at her dressing-table, studying her image in the mirror. Her face was fully made up although she wore a dressing-gown. She turned to her niece. 'What do you think? Is this good? Or too much for a lunch?' But as soon as Rosetta looked at Marie she no longer expected a second opinion about cosmetics. 'Marie?' Rosetta said. 'What's wrong?'

Marie's uneven breathing broke into sobs. Rosetta rose from her stool and enveloped Marie in her arms. The sobbing continued but decreased in intensity. The older woman led her niece to the edge of the bed and they sat. 'What's wrong?' Rosetta asked.

'I . . .' Marie began, but her gulps returned.

'There, there,' Rosetta said.

'I . . .' Marie began again. 'I *hate* men! Just when you're doing what you think they want, they change their minds and decide to do without you at the last minute. They throw you off like . . . like a caterpillar! I hate them! I hate them!'


Despite the light of a full moon Gina and Angelo did not take the riverside path after they returned their car to its garage. This time they walked up the road to Walcot Street. But instead of going home they continued along the street until they were on the opposite side from the Shaylers'. There they stopped. They looked at the house. Only a dim light showed, on the upper floor.

Gina looked at her watch. 'She'll be reading, and he's about to bring his Horlicks to bed.'

'Unless this is a water night,' Angelo said. 'And God help the washing-up liquid.'

Then Gina heard a rustle in the shadows behind her. She turned and saw a figure emerge.

'Did you get my message?' David said. 'Is that why you're here?'




The Old Man was restless. Having slept better the previous night – after all that wine – he wasn't particularly sleepy now, despite the approach of bedtime. 'I feel like a sandwich,' he said. 'You got any sandwich?'

Mama looked up from her knitting.

'I know. Prosciutto. That's what I feel like.'

'It's not what you look like,' Mama said.

'Ha very ha.'

'I'll have to go down,' Mama said. 'There's none up here.'

Some nights the Old Man would have said he'd make do with whatever was in their own fridge. Tonight he said, 'Me too, I'll come down.'

'Suit yourself,' Mama said, lowering her knitting resignedly.

They were somewhat surprised to find the downstairs kitchen empty. The Old Man looked at the clock. 'Huh!' he said. These days they all stayed up all night. It used to be that ten was bedtime, ten thirty snoring. Stay out till midnight, you expected someone to call for the police. No longer. Not now. They should have grown up in the village he and Mama had grown up in. 'Huh!' he said again.

The Old Man seated himself and watched as Mama held the bread against her chest and cut it. She made the bread herself because she knew he didn't like soft English muck. Mama had taken to English life but at least, thank God, not that.

She finished with the bread and began her work with the ham. He could smell it. Good. He was trying to decide something to say, something she would like, when they both heard footsteps in the passage.

'Company we got,' the Old Man said.

The company, surprisingly, was Salvatore.

'What's this on a Friday night?' Mama asked. 'You're all right? Is Muffin with you?'

'I'm alone,' Salvatore said. 'I went to the office first. The light's on, and the new computer's going crazy, but nobody's there. There's a message, from David. It says he's gone to watch outside the Shaylers'. Mrs Shayler rang. She says her husband is panicking.'

'That poor woman,' Mama said.

'So are Gina and Angelo around?' Salvatore asked. 'Did they get back from Howard?'

'We just came down,' Mama said with a shrug.

'So nobody's around?' Salvatore asked.

'I'm around,' the Old Man said. 'But I don't count. Huh!'

'Are you going to wait, Salvatore?' Mama asked.

'I suppose so, Mama.' Salvatore sat at the table. 'You do count, Papa.'

'Nice sandwich?' Mama said. 'Prosciutto?'

'Don't do me any favours,' the Old Man said.

'No thanks, Mama,' Salvatore said. 'I just had some cheese on toast.'

'And where was that?' Mama asked. 'They serve such things at your Rose and Crown pub?'

Having been offered a simple explanation Salvatore preferred it to the hazards of the accurate one. 'Yes,' he said.

'So what business?' the Old Man said. 'More Shaylers?'

'Look at this,' Salvatore said, passing his father the photograph of Kit Bridges that the slimy detective had given to Bonnie the Regular.

'Nice-looking girl,' the Old Man said. He looked at his son. 'The model kind?'

They all heard the door open at street level. Mama went to the top of the stairs. 'Gina, Angelo and David,' she reported.

The Old Man said, 'The excitement starts, everybody shows up. Should I call Rosetta in here? And Marie?'

'Rosetta has her beauty sleep,' Mama said. 'Leave the girl in peace.'


In her desperation to distract Marie, Rosetta had led her niece to the new computer. In her desperation to be distracted, Marie had paid attention as her aunt turned the machine on and began to bring images to the screen. The first thing Rosetta and Marie did together was leave an electronic message in David's 'mail box'. Marie provided rude text.

'I'm surprised David isn't answering,' Rosetta said. 'The other station is turned on.'

'He can count, but he can't read,' Marie said acidly.

'He must be able to read "Letter for David",' Rosetta said. 'That's what should be flashing on his screen.'

'He's probably going crazy because *he* doesn't know how to use the electronic mail box,' Marie said. 'He doesn't, does he?'

'No,' Rosetta said. 'We only worked with the graphics last night.'

'I can just see him twitching because he doesn't know what to do. Let's leave him another message.'

'All right,' Rosetta said.

'I wish Jenny had one of these,' Marie said. 'It would be mega to send messages. And we could do homework together without either of us having to leave the house. It's not like a computer at all.'


'On the back,' Salvatore said.

The Old Man turned the picture over. '"Clint," it says. And a telephone number. So?'

'Look at the number,' Salvatore said.

The Old Man looked. 'This number,' he said. 'I know this from somewhere.'

'Good, Papa, good,' Salvatore said. 'Show Angelo.'

The Old Man handed the picture across the table. Gina and Angelo studied the back. Angelo said, 'But that's the same number Jack Shayler has been ringing.'

'Exactly!' Salvatore said.

'But that means,' Gina said, 'that the slimy detective is Howard the Printer.'

# 12

Shortly after eight in the morning, Gina left the house to walk to the Shaylers'. A post-midnight decision had established her lost pet as a carrot-coloured canary named Jasper. It was also decided that she must knock on the door of the house next door first, to establish credibility in case Jack Shayler was watching the street.

Considering the early hour on a Saturday morning the Shaylers' neighbour was surprisingly civil. 'Ay, luv, I used to keep cage-birds myself,' a robust old man in braces told Gina when she explained about her missing canary. 'Happiest days of my life, birding days. But the little buggers can be the very devil when they get out. Don't give up hope, though, luv. Delicate they may be, but sometimes surprisingly hardy. You never quite know what to expect from a canary.'

Gina gave the good neighbour a prepared sheet with fictional facts about Jasper and her non-fictional telephone number. Although it was all typed out, the man insisted on getting his specs before he was willing to conclude the interview. 'Right then, luv,' he said when he was finally secure about the details. 'I'll keep my beak up against the window looking out for the little fellow. That's a promise.'

Gina proceeded next door. The reasoning that led to Jasper the Canary instead of, say, Jasper the Tortoise was that it would be easier for Mrs Shayler. She could pick a moment to go to the window and declare, 'Look, there's Jasper!' That a canary would not still be visible when her husband came to the window was entirely reasonable. Even so, Mrs Shayler would have to ring Gina to report the sighting. That's what good neighbours did.

Once on the telephone, Gina could ask Mrs Shayler yes-or-no questions. Are you all right? Can you come and see me? Do you want us to follow if your husband goes somewhere?

It was not the surest plan in the world, but it was the best the late-night gathering had come up with in response to 'You'd better think of some reason to come round here in the morning,' as reported by David.

With any luck Jasper the Canary would also give Gina a chance to see their client and make sure she was all right. Not that anyone thought Jack Shayler would injure her. But if he was 'panicking', who knew? The message that David had recorded so faithfully was a disturbing one.

Gina walked up the Shaylers' short path slowly. She was nervous. But in the event the door opened before she rang the bell. It revealed Mrs Shayler standing inside. Mrs Shayler looked extremely tired.

However, before Gina could speak, Mrs Shayler raised a finger to her lips. The meaning was, 'Don't say anything.' Gina nodded, and then, with more boldness than Gina would have expected, Mrs Shayler stepped outside the house and drew the door shut behind her.

Gina whispered, 'Are you all right?'

'Oh yes,' Mrs Shayler said and then, as Gina watched, Mrs Shayler's grey and sleepless face was transformed by a smile. 'It's all come out,' she said. 'Everything. It's wonderful. I'm so happy.'

It was the last message that Gina expected. All she could say was, 'So, what's it about?'

But Mrs Shayler said quietly, 'He's asleep. I'd better go in now. I don't want him to wake up and me not be there.'

Gina said, 'Ring or visit as soon as you get a chance.'

But Mrs Shayler disappeared into the house and closed the door without promising, or even acknowledging that she had heard Gina's request.

Gina stood for seconds on the doorstep, trying to absorb what had happened. When finally she turned to leave, she realized that she had not given Mrs Shayler the sheet she had prepared with the phone number and Jasper's description.

No point sticking it through the letter box. By itself it was meaningless.

'It's all come out. Everything. It's wonderful. I'm so happy.' Gina couldn't make sense of *that* at all.

She set off toward home, but she had made only a few yards' progress when the Shaylers' neighbour opened his door and hailed her. 'Missus,' the old man in braces called. 'Ayup, missus!' He beckoned her to return to his door and Gina could do nothing but accede to his wish.

In confiding tones the man said, 'I saw how she turned you away next door, and now you're heading home. You mustn't give up, luv. They're an odd pair, them two. But don't take it to heart. If you give me that sheet of paper, I'll see they get it before the day's out.' The man nodded and winked. 'Stand by me,' he said. 'Mustn't despair.'

There was nothing Gina could do but give the good neighbour the page of details about Jasper the Canary.


Marie woke early by her own Saturday standards because there were things to arrange. She never set an alarm clock. If ever she needed to wake up early, she woke up early. She didn't understand people for whom such things were a problem. Neither did she understand why her parents, grandparents and brother were seated around the table when she appeared in the kitchen.

'It's all come out? It's wonderful? I'm so happy?' Angelo was saying. 'I don't understand. What can the woman mean?'

'Morning, Marie,' Gina said.

'What are you all talking about?' Marie asked.

'It's another satisfied customer,' the Old Man said.

'But what do we do now?' Angelo said.

'Mum? Dad?'

'Shut up,' David said. 'It's business. You wouldn't understand.'

'A lot *you* know,' Marie said. '*You* don't even know how to open your electronic mail box.'

'Children!' Gina said. 'Don't interrupt!'

Marie busied herself with a crumpet. David's attention was

now split because of his sister's unexpected challenge. He didn't know which issue to follow.

'What's the "do now"?' the Old Man said. 'Does she owe you money?'

'No,' Angelo said.

'So "now" you "do" nothing, that's what you do now. You've got a happy customer who paid the bill. What more do you want?'

'But we don't know what's happened, Papa,' Gina said. 'Mrs Shayler may be satisfied, but we don't know how we satisfied her.'

'You got hired,' the Old Man said. 'You worked. You got paid. The customer is happy. Do you think the client has to explain all your little curiosities? No, no.'

'But it is a puzzle,' Mama said. 'Give them that.'

'I give them whatever they want,' the Old Man said. 'That's my mistake.'

'But it's such a turn-around from the phone call Mrs Shayler made to David last night,' Gina said.

'She wanted you to go to her house in the morning. You went to her house. Now the husband is asleep and the client says everything is good,' the Old Man said. 'Things happen.'

'I don't know that we *can* do anything,' Angelo said.

'If you do a thing, who pays?' the Old Man asked, an element of exasperation entering his voice.

'Have more coffee,' Mama said, 'and let the children decide for themselves.'

'Huh!' the Old Man said. He held out his mug.

There was a pause. Marie said, 'Dad?'

'What is it, Marie?'

'You know you said you had a job for me?'

Angelo stared at his daughter.

'A job today,' Marie said. 'Don't you remember?'

'Ah,' Angelo said.

'Well, I've decided I'd like to do it.'

'What job?' David asked.

'I thought you had to go to Jenny's. I thought it was urgent,' Angelo said.

'Well, I'm going to see her tonight instead,' Marie said. 'And I need the money.'

'What for does a young girl need money?' the Old Man said. 'Are you cold? Are you hungry?'

'I've got fashion statements to make, Grandad,' Marie said with a bright smile.

'Fashion, is it?' the Old Man said. 'Fashion *burns* money. I should know.' He looked in the direction of Rosetta's room. 'Me too, I had a daughter.'

'What job?' David insisted. 'Why have you offered dopey Marie a job and not me?'

'*You* don't even know how to open your electronic mail box,' Marie said. '*That's* why.'

'Dad?' David said. 'Mum?'

At that moment Rosetta entered. 'Hello, everybody,' she said.

'Good morning, Aunt Rosetta!' Marie said, and she ran to her aunt and hugged her. Everyone noticed the action as an unusual one except David.

David said, 'I want to know about this job! I did well last night, didn't I?'

'Very well,' Gina said.

'There are jobs for you both,' Angelo said. 'Don't worry. Come to the office. Give me an hour.'

'Isn't it a *fabulous* day!' Rosetta said.


Gina and Angelo sat in the office drinking tea. 'I thought Papa was going to insist on a job too,' Angelo said. 'Sometimes life has too many hands. I can't keep up with the complications.' He took a garibaldi from the biscuit plate. 'These don't have the taste they used to have. Do you think?'

'So why take another?' Gina asked.

'I don't know,' Angelo said. He considered putting the biscuit back. He bit into it instead. 'No, they're not like I remember them.'

'So what are these jobs you're going to give the children?'

'What I told Marie was I needed someone to follow Jack Shayler. So I suppose it's follow Jack Shayler.'

103

'Might be interesting,' Gina said.

'But . . .' Angelo began.

They finished together, 'Who pays?' and laughed.

'But tell me, what's with Marie *now*?' Angelo asked. 'Is "easy money" not so easy, or is it just postponed? She says tonight's with Jenny. So is that a lie? Is it Easy Money Terry tonight? Is that it? Tell me.'

'She goes out with Jenny most Saturdays,' Gina said. 'You know that.'

'I used to know it,' Angelo said. 'Now I don't know what I know.' He displayed his garibaldi. 'These used to have taste. Or is it me? She says she's going out. What else could it be?'

'Leave it,' Gina said.

'But I'm not a satisfied customer.'

'There's nothing we can do, Angelo. We have to wait and see.'

Angelo studied his once-bitten biscuit. He couldn't put it back but that didn't mean he had to finish it. 'I suppose.'

'What job are you going to give to David?'

'Follow Marie tonight?'

Gina said nothing.

Angelo said, 'I thought I'd tell him to follow Rosetta's man after lunch. See if he's married.'

'You can't do that!' Gina said, feeling that she had to respond to this 'joke' because she had not responded to the first one.

Angelo smiled because Gina had been lured into thinking he was making a serious suggestion. Just because he was confused about Marie didn't mean he'd gone stupid. 'But I've got to give him something,' he said.


'Rosetta is so happy today,' Mama said. 'Did you notice?'

'Of course,' the Old Man said.

Of course *not*, Mama thought. But I can't expect miracles at his age. She decided to change the subject. 'For a minute I thought Angelo was going to ask *you* to work today. He seems very busy.'

'If he needs me, he knows who he can count on,' the Old Man said, but despite himself he yawned.

104

'We were all up very late last night,' Mama said. 'We haven't done that for a long time.'

'No,' the Old Man agreed. He stroked his chin. 'No.'

He's going to reminisce, Mama thought. I hope not Norman Stiles.

But the Old Man surprised her. 'Rosetta so happy,' he said.

'It's good to see,' Mama said. 'She's been sad.'

'Does that mean her Walter is back?' the Old Man asked.

Oh, Mama thought, disappointed. 'No.'

'Walter,' the Old Man said. 'That would be handy for the will.'

'Don't be silly,' Mama said.

'Now I'm silly? What's silly? He's a solicitor, right, this Walter?'

'To think you're going to cut Salvatore out of your will is silly,' Mama said.

The Old Man looked at her. 'Who said that?'

'I know what you think, and such a thing about poor Salvatore . . . Ridiculous! You're a foolish old man and you shouldn't interfere in the children's lives.'

'Foolish it is now? Huh! You're hungry, I'm so foolish? You're starving, I'm so foolish?'

'You're just causing trouble because you can't accept that there are things more important to Salvatore than the business which was everything to you. Because you can't accept you're not so important to the business any more yourself. That's the truth of it.'

'Huh!' the Old Man said. 'Huh!'

'Time to adjust,' Mama said. 'Act your age. Grow up.'

'Huh!'

Mama sighed. Oh dear. He was bound to sulk now.

'Huh!'

They sat in silence for a while. Then Mama said, 'I was thinking.'

Some miracle, the Old Man thought.

'About the Shaylers.'

The Old Man hesitated but couldn't resist. 'What about the Shaylers? They're foolish too?'

'How suddenly they're happy,' Mama said.

'Like Rosetta,' the Old Man said. 'Everybody's happy. Happy-happy. It's catching, maybe.'

'I think maybe it's common enemy,' Mama said.

'What nonsense are you talking?' Savouring 'nonsense'.

'Why the wife is satisfied today.'

'OK, so why?'

'Yesterday Angelo and Salvatore frightened the husband. He thinks they're killers, my boys. So the husband runs home, cries on the shoulder. Panics, she said. So maybe also the husband confides, "Boo-hoo. This has been happening, that has been happening."'

'What happening?'

'All why he cried for help with the washing-up liquid.'

The Old Man considered. 'He could confide,' he conceded.

'And then the wife takes his side, no matter what,' Mama said. 'So now they are together against whatever it is. The common enemy. So suddenly she's happy, because between them there's no more division.'

The Old Man sat silent.

'You don't think it can work like that? Because I tell you, it can.'

The Old Man said, 'You could be right.'

'Such a vote of confidence,' Mama said, but she was not displeased.

'Give me a paper, I'll mark an "X" so I vote for you, if that's what you want,' he said. 'Everybody gets what they want. What else am I for? Salvatore wants to freeload, be my guest. You want a vote, here give me a pencil. Huh!'

Mama studied her husband. Though he was old in so many ways, he remained responsive to reason. She rose from her chair.

He watched her closely. 'No pencil?'

If only he could ever be brought to apply himself to *important* things, Mama thought. 'Let me get you something. Tea?'

'All right, tea,' he said.

*

Although Angelo was still sitting by the window when David and Marie arrived, he was on the telephone. The children stood waiting, but their father hung up without saying anything.

'Not there?' Gina asked from across the table.

'Not there.'

'And no machine?' Gina said.

'He's never met Rosetta's friend.'

'What do you want to do? Wait till Monday?'

Angelo considered. 'I think it's worth a trip this morning. Howard may not be there, but other places in the row might be open. Someone might know things. Even where he lives.'

'Good idea,' Gina said.

'I'll go.'

'No,' Gina said. 'You stay here and run your ops.' She rose and handed Angelo her empty tea mug. Then she picked up the telephone and put it back on the desk.

'Huh!' Angelo said.

'Bye,' Gina said to them all, and she left.

As the door closed, Marie said, 'Reporting for duty.'

David, who still felt hard done by, said nothing.

Angelo said, 'It's the Shaylers. We're worried.'

'See, I *told* you I was following Mr Shayler,' Marie said to her brother. David made a face in reply.

'If you're going to squabble,' Angelo said, 'go back to the house. This is work. Either be professional or go away to play your games. Am I understood?'

Both children nodded. 'Who do I follow?' David asked. 'Or is it something else?'

'I want a tail on each of them. Marie, I want you to follow Mrs Shayler if she comes out. David, Mr Shayler. That way round nobody ends up where it's obvious, like Marie in a men's shop or David in dresses.' Then he described the two Shaylers. 'Got it?'

'Yes, Dad,' Marie said.

David said, 'Do you know where they might go?'

'Our problem is we don't know. Suddenly the Shaylers are confusing.'

'Got it,' David said.

'I want a proper job,' Angelo said. 'Everything in the notebook with times. Phone in regularly. This is work. Not . . .' Angelo hesitated over the phrase 'easy money'. He opted instead to say, 'This is not money for nothing.'

The children nodded.

'And nothing even slightly dangerous,' Angelo said emphatically. 'I can't imagine what, but Shayler tells his wife someone wants to kill him. Maybe that's just because your Uncle Sal is so ugly, but he might have some other reason. So you only follow if he walks, David. No bus. No taxi. And that's for you too with the wife, Marie.'

'OK, Dad,' both children said.

'And if they stay inside all day, I still need who goes in, who goes out.' Angelo checked his watch. 'You work till six. Phone in every hour. One can call for both unless you separate. Got it?'

'Yes, Dad,' the detectives said.

'On your way.'

They left.

Angelo moved to the window. The flower-dotted backs of the Paragon crescent smiled from above, but he looked down to the street. He waited for his children to emerge on to the pavement and turn in the direction of the Shaylers' house. They did, and he saw Marie toss her hair the way she often did after she said something she thought was funny. Then he saw David poke the end of Marie's shoulder with his fist. Then he lost sight of them, though he stood gazing down the street in the direction they had gone.


Rosetta popped into the kitchen looking for Gina but didn't find her. The car keys were not on their hook, so maybe Gina was out.

Or maybe not. Humming to herself Rosetta used her hips to flip her skirt from one hall wall to the other as she walked through to the office. After knocking perfunctorily, she went in.

Angelo was standing at the window. He turned.

'Is Gina around?' Rosetta asked.

'No,' Angelo said. 'Is there business?'

Rosetta swirled for her brother. 'What do you think?' She wore a full black skirt and a white blouse. Her cheeks were red, a combination of natural and artificial colourings.

'Wow!' Angelo said, recognizing what was being asked for, and having no difficulty about providing it. 'You look great!'

Rosetta beamed. 'Do you really think so?'

'I really think so,' Angelo said with enthusiasm. 'Where is he taking you, this equipment giant?'

'Hardly a giant,' Rosetta said. She pirouetted. 'Do you know the French café in Shires Yard?'

'You'll knock 'em dead, *ma jolie soeur.*'

'Oh Angelo, thank you for saying so!' Rosetta went to her brother and kissed him. 'Oh dear. Now you've got lipstick on your cheek.' Humming, she left him to go back to her room.

Angelo rubbed his cheek. Now I have lipstick on my hand, he thought.

He returned to the window to see if he could see the children. He shouldn't be able to, but . . . Neither Marie nor David was in sight. Angelo tested the soil around the base of each plant on the sill. All were moist.

He looked at the plate of biscuits. He picked up a garibaldi. Perhaps this one had the taste they ought to have. But instead of biting, Angelo dropped the biscuit back on the plate. *Basta!* Enough chances he'd given them. He picked up the plate and scooped the biscuits back into their box. He gathered up his and Gina's tea mugs. Time to do something constructive.

At that moment he heard a clatter of feet on the stairs from the street. He heard a high-pitched voice, but not the words. The bustle meant it was the children. Coming to the office? What for? Some argument?

Angelo stood, facing the door squarely. Resolved to fire his 'ops' on the spot. *Basta* was *basta*, no?

The office door burst open. Kit Bridges marched in. She was followed by a round man with a camera hanging by a strap from his neck. 'This is him,' Kit Bridges said. She pointed at Angelo.

109

# 13

Gina parked and walked to Block Letter having decided to force her way into the premises if she could do so without attracting attention. She didn't know quite what she would look for, but she felt strongly that she needed to know what Howard the Slimy Detective was printing that could possibly affect Jack Shayler.

But while Block Letter was not open for business on a Saturday morning, some of the other small companies beneath the arches were. Many, Gina saw, dealt with aspects of the motor trade, though one was a monumental mason. There was also clear activity under an arch that adjoined Block Letter's, although there was nothing to indicate the nature of the business. A van was parked in front of it, and doors of both van and premises were open.

Gina tried Block Letter itself first. She knocked, she rattled the door, she peered through the plastic window. But nothing elicited response.

So Gina went next door. Inside she found a man and two women busily preparing sandwiches. The two women each had a table covered with rolls and fillings. The man gathered and bagged the completed sandwiches from both tables and allocated them to flat boxes. Behind the women were more rolls and tubs of fillings. The quantity of food being prepared was huge.

'Sorry, love,' one of the women said as Gina came in. 'No time to stop and sell you a bap.'

'It's information I was hoping for,' Gina said.

'If it's a one-off event you're organizing, we won't be able to fit you in till week after next. If it's something regular, give us the dates and we'll put you on the circuit. If you're desperate, we can probably get someone over to you for next Saturday, long as you're not too far from another sale we're already catering.' The woman spoke without missing so much as a tomato slice.

The second woman said, 'We stock you to sell yourself. We don't provide counter staff or display. But our rolls are top quality, and if people like the food you provide they always stay longer and buy more.'

'If it's for an event during the week,' the man said, 'great. But if it's another bloody weekend or bank holiday gig, we're already up to our boiled eggs.'

'He means "eyeballs", love. But he's right,' the first woman said. 'We're very busy, thank God.'

'Does that cover what you wanted to know?' the second woman said.

'I'm afraid I've come in about something else altogether,' Gina said.

'What would that be?' the man asked.

'I'm trying to get a word with the bloke who runs the printers next door.'

'Oh,' the second woman said. '*Him.*'

'You know him then?' Gina asked.

'Not to be civil to. Ten seconds after I said hello the first time, he was trying it on,' the second woman said.

'Ugly git with a flash car? That who you mean?' the man said.

'He's the only one who works there, Karl,' the first woman said.

'I thought there was two of them,' Karl said.

'Not for months now,' the second woman said. 'Ever since the murder.'


The round man with the camera said, 'Miss Bridges has told me all about this mystery man who's posing as one of your private detectives, Mr Lunghi. So what I'd like to do is take a photograph of you and Miss Bridges together so they can run it with the story.'

'Hang on,' Angelo said. 'What story?'

'In the *Chronicle*,' the man with the camera said.

'Oh please, Mr Lunghi,' Kit Bridges said. 'I can't have some evil crustacean going around the city suggesting that there's something in my life that needs investigating.'

'A story in the paper will help track the bugger down,' the man with the camera said.

'I'm not sure that's the right way to go about it,' Angelo said.

The man with the camera said, 'The paper will run the story anyway, but with a picture it'll get better play. And it will be good publicity for you, Mr Lunghi. The *Chronicle*'s read all over the area. A story with a pic will bring in more business than any advertising you can do. Chances are you'll be rushed off your feet. I've seen it happen before.'

'And it will be good for me too,' Kit Bridges said. 'I'll be on record saying that this sub-human is telling lies about me.'

'So why not a picture just of you?' Angelo said.

'Much better the two of you,' the man with the camera said. '"Private eye rescues damsel in distress." They'll print it four times as big. Could even be on the front page if it's a slow news day.'

'Oh please, Mr Lunghi,' Kit Bridges said. 'Please!'

The man with the camera said, 'You wouldn't want to disappoint the pretty lady, now would you, Mr Lunghi?'

'Well . . .' Angelo said.

'That's great! Now tell me, Mr Lunghi, you must have a mac around somewhere. And a hat with a brim. The sort of thing you might wear when you're out on a case. And how about a gun? Needn't be the real thing. And do put those dirty cups down.'

'No costumes,' Angelo said. 'No dressing up. If the intention of this picture isn't serious, I'm not interested.'

'Of course, Mr Lunghi, if that's your feeling we'll respect it completely,' the round man with the camera said.

Angelo thought about Howard's use of Kit Bridges' photograph to try to pick up women. Maybe even planning to harm them. Warning women in the city, that would be a good thing to do. 'All right, then,' he said, 'let's do it.'

The man with the camera pushed some buttons and held his camera up. He said, 'Let's sit you in the chair by the window.'

Angelo hesitated. 'Shouldn't I be at my desk?'

'It's less formal if you're in the chair,' the man with the camera said. 'Miss Bridges, dump those cups somewhere.'

Angelo allowed Kit Bridges to take the mugs. Oh well. The picture would show a friendly, family business. Angelo sat in the chair. Kit Bridges put the mugs by the computer.

'Now, Miss Bridges,' the man with the camera said, 'how about giving him a thank-you kiss? Bending over, like they do on seaside postcards. You know the drill.'

'Hang on,' Angelo said, but Kit Bridges immediately moved in close, bent sharply at the waist and put her lips on Angelo's cheek while rotating her torso toward the camera in a way which maximized the display of her cleavage. The flash went off twice in rapid succession.

'That was nice,' the man with the camera said. 'Now how about sitting on his lap?'

'I'm not very heavy,' Kit Bridges said. She jumped on to Angelo's lap.

From the doorway to the street Angelo heard Salvatore's voice. 'Well well, bubba, what have we here?'

As Angelo turned to look at his brother, he came face to face with Kit Bridges. Kit Bridges kissed him full on the lips. The flash went off twice again.

'That's *great!*' the round man with the camera said. 'That astonished look was perfect, Mr Lunghi. You're a natural.'


Saturday parking in the centre of Bath lived up to its reputation. Gina found a queue at the Ham Gardens multi-storey. The railway station was hopeless. Manvers Street was full. It was particularly frustrating to drive past the very building she wanted to go into without being able to stop.

As she waited at the lights by the Abbey Gina had a decision to make. Circle to try the car-parks again? Or would it end up quicker to drive home and walk?

She opted to try for space one more time. She drove the circuit that took her back to the car-parks. And her persistence was rewarded. Not only had the Ham Gardens queue cleared, when she drove in she was able to snap up a first-floor place as it was vacated by a dirty white van. An early bird.

Gina paid, displayed, and walked to the police station.


'Excellent bone structure,' Salvatore said after Kit Bridges and the man with the camera left to rush the photographs to the newspaper. 'Even better than on the picture Howard shows.'

'A story in the paper will warn women to be wary,' Angelo said.

'Is that what you said to get her on your lap?'

'If you ever need tips on handling women,' Angelo said, 'you know where to come.'

'How did Gina do at the Shaylers' this morning?'

'Sally, can we talk over a cup of coffee outside?' Angelo said.

'Any particular reason?'

'I want to have a look at how David and Marie are getting along.'


Gina knew enough police officers in Bath for it to be almost certain that one of them would be on duty. But it was Charlie she asked for and Charlie she got.

A constable escorted her to the door of the computer services room. Gina knocked and went in. Charlie was at his desk, talking to a woman CID officer. The woman said, 'If only girls were a Diamond's best friend.' She rose and offered Gina her chair. 'See you later,' the woman said to Charlie.

'I'll warn you when he's prowling around if you'll warn me,' Charlie said. The woman laughed and left.

Gina sat.

Charlie said, 'Gina! We talk so often but meet so rarely. Who's been murdered?'

'That's what I hope you'll tell me,' Gina said.

\*

'I was just about to send David to ring you,' Marie said.

'Uncle Sal and I were passing,' Angelo said. 'How are you getting on? Has anything happened?'

'Nothing,' Marie said.

'The postman delivered a letter,' David said. He looked at his notebook. 'At 10.48. Buff envelope.'

'He doesn't want to know that,' Marie said.

'Keep up the good work,' Salvatore said. 'Come on, bubba.'

Outside a coffee shop called The Underground, Salvatore stopped. But Angelo said, 'Not here. If they're busy they take forever.'

Salvatore shrugged. 'Great loos.'

'What?'

'The walls are papered with comics.'

Angelo led his brother to a catering van in the yard outside the brick warehouse which housed the Saturday Walcot Street antiques fair. 'I'm buying,' he said.

'In that case,' Salvatore said, 'a large coffee and . . . Those filled rolls look good.'

'And a tea for me,' Angelo said.

They sat on white plastic chairs by the van. Salvatore said, 'Surveillance on the Shaylers, eh?'

'It's a long story,' Angelo said.

'Before you start, have you or Gina heard from Muffin?'

'Muffin?'

'She was going to try modelling for me this morning. But she didn't show up, and there was no message. And now she's not at her hotel. I thought maybe . . .'

'I haven't heard from her,' Angelo said. 'Might she be in trouble? Is that what you think?'

'I'm surprised, that's all. She seemed so organized,' Salvatore said. 'And I'm really in the mood to get some work done.'

'Oh, *that* kind of modelling,' Angelo said.


'It's the romance of computers,' Charlie said. 'Press a few buttons, and locate a murder.' He read from the screen. 'Adamson, the dead man's name is?'

'That's the name I was given,' Gina said.

'Well, let's see what we can come up with.'

In a few moments a file came up on Charlie's screen. 'Right first time,' he said. 'Murder it was. Blow to the head. Unsolved.' He turned from the screen. 'Gina, just what's brought you in to ask about this?'

When Angelo got back to the office there were no signs of Gina's having returned from Block Letter. He sat at his desk. Nothing on the answering machine. Then he noticed that the computer terminal was on.

Had he left it on? No, he hadn't looked at it all morning. So David must have left it on overnight. Ah, David had taken the late call from Mrs Shayler and rushed out.

Angelo saw that there was a flashing box on the screen which included the message, 'Letter for David.' What was that supposed to mean?

Angelo's instinct was to turn the terminal off, but if he did that maybe something would be irretrievably lost. He considered ringing through to Rosetta. But Rosetta was bound to have left for her lunch. And even if she hadn't, Angelo didn't much feel like being the recipient of a computer lesson, even one not conducted by Ignatius White.

Angelo tried to ignore the computer. But that was hard too, what with it flashing at him so insistently. He put his hand over the flashing box on the computer's screen, as if to make it go away. Only then did he remember having seen television reports about computers that would respond to touch. But this one didn't. At least Rosetta hadn't bought *that*. Yet.

Angelo noticed the computer's 'mouse'. He pushed it and it clicked. Angelo looked at the screen. Nothing had happened. He pushed on the mouse again. It clicked again. Nothing happened again.

Then Angelo rolled the mouse easily around its pad. A flashing symbol, more like a spot than anything else, moved as the mouse moved. Angelo manoeuvred the flashing spot into the flashing box, thinking that maybe somehow they would cancel each other out and give him relief.

But the flashing continued. With nothing particular in mind, Angelo pushed on the mouse and made it click. The screen burst into life and it displayed a letter addressed to David.

Angelo felt distinctly pleased with himself. He must have 'opened' the 'mail box'. And although the 'letter' was to David, Angelo read it. It wasn't as if it was a real letter.

Dear David, How astute of you to be able to receive this letter, but then you *would* be able to, because it's a machine. Give you anything *human* and you'd *kill* it, and don't say you wouldn't. I was there for that jar of woodlice when you were six, don't forget. *And* when you tried eating ants to see what they tasted like. But the main reason you'd *kill* anything is that you're a *man*. Not a real man. You'll probably never be a *real* man but you're male and that's bad enough. EVERYTHING MALE IS SCUMMY, DUMMY, AND THAT INCLUDES YOU! Your loving sister, Marie-the-Free-*Esprit*. Mega-death to all things *male* in the universe.

Salvatore couldn't find a bell, so he knocked using the letter box. He rapped several times and was about to give up when the door opened. 'You?' Bonnie the Regular said.

'Good morning.' Salvatore looked at his watch. 'Good early afternoon.'

'What's the matter? Your sister throw you out?'

'I need a model,' Salvatore said.

'Well, I don't need a private detective,' Bonnie said, and she slammed the door.

Having read the letter once, Angelo read it again and the net effect was to be pleased. Marie's displeasure with the male half of the species seemed more general than anything aimed solely at David. And that was good because Easy Money Terry was unquestionably male.

Then the telephone rang. Who? One of his ops? 'Angelo Lunghi.'

'Oh,' a man's voice said. 'I were expecting a lady. What number's that?'

Angelo recited the telephone number.

'Ay, that's it,' the man said. 'This morning a young lady gave me this number because she lost her canary.'

'Ah,' Angelo said.

'Thing is, see, I may just have spotted her Jasper here in my back garden. I wondered if she wanted to come round and have a look.'

'The young lady isn't here at the moment,' Angelo said. 'But I'll give her the message as soon as I see her.'

'Ay,' the man said with some disappointment, 'you do that. I'll go back to me window and see if I can spot the little rascal again. It were only a glimpse I got. Wouldn't want to raise the young lady's hopes just to dash 'em again.'

When he had hung up, Angelo looked around the desk for the message pad. The pad wasn't where it was supposed to be. What Angelo found instead were David's cartoons, left from last night.

Angelo picked the top cartoon up. He hadn't realized that David could draw so well. He studied the cartoon and was impressed.

Of course Gina had talent that way, though it was not much in evidence since she'd dropped out of college. And maybe David had also benefited from some of the same genes that produced Salvatore's artistic talents. Angelo smiled. Papa wouldn't like that.

Then his smile faded. For a moment he considered just how much David's papa would like it.

But Angelo didn't get much time to think about his own feelings. Beneath the cartoon he noticed a message card, one which had already been filled in.

He picked it up and read that last night Muffin had rung, from a pay phone, uncertain whether she would get back to her hotel or not. She had wanted to speak to Gina.

# 14

When Charlie got off the phone he said, 'Varden was on his way to lunch, but he'll stop here first.'

'Thanks,' Gina said. 'Especially for the personal endorsement.'

'I hope it was embarrassing to listen to,' Charlie said.

'What's this Varden like?'

'Ambitious,' Charlie said.

Moments later a tall, craggy-faced man in his early thirties entered the room after a perfunctory knock. 'Ah, Roger,' Charlie said. 'This is Gina Lunghi.'

'My pleasure, Mrs Lunghi,' Varden said as he and Gina shook hands. 'Charlie tells me you're a private detective and that you have an interest in the Adamson murder.' Varden's voice was rich, low and Scottish.

'And Charlie tells me that you were involved in the investigation,' Gina said.

'I still am, should there be developments.' Varden raised thin eyebrows.

'Shall I confess now?'

'Oh no,' Varden said. 'Take more time about it. I like my wee fish to wriggle on the hook.'

'In that case I'm only here to get background,' Gina said.

'That's better,' Varden said. 'Now, Lunghi is an Italian name, is it not?'

'Yes,' Gina said.

'Grand. I love Italian food. And I'm very hungry.'


When Gina did not appear in the office by one, Angelo went across to the house and made himself a sandwich. But it didn't look nearly as good as the roll he'd bought for Salvatore. For a moment Angelo considered going out to buy a roll for himself.

It would be an excuse to look in on David and Marie again. But the impulse passed. Angelo ate his sandwich and stayed put.

His only lunchtime contact with the outside world came by telephone. 'David Lunghi reporting at 13.28, Dad,' David said. 'The Shaylers are still in their house.'

'Everything's straightforward?'

'People keep stopping to talk to Marie.'

'Strangers?'

'No. Kids from school. She doesn't pay half the attention to the job that she should.'

Angelo didn't know how best to respond to David's high moral tone. Fire Marie? And leave her free to pursue alternative activities? Hardly. Yet there was David's sense of grievance to account for.

However David read his father's hesitation and said, 'Still, I suppose if there's a group of kids around, we don't stand out so much.'

'I think you're right,' Angelo said.

But later, after he returned to the office, Angelo suddenly felt that he should have told David that he was doing well as a detective.

Suppose David did decide to take up a different career, artistic or otherwise. The truth of the matter was that the possibility had never seriously crossed Angelo's mind before. David was always so keen, so eager to take part in business. The problem was to contain his enthusiasm, to keep him from neglecting his studies. But what can you ever count on, in this world, in this day and age?

'Huh!' Angelo said. And for once he was aware of the similarity between his position and that of his father.

But Angelo's musings were interrupted. He heard the street door open. He heard steps on the stairs. Not Kit Bridges again, surely. He had a thing or two to say to that young woman, now that he had reflected on how she had manipulated him to get herself some publicity.

But the steps were slow, hesitant. Mrs Shayler? But would Mrs Shayler be hesitant now? Wouldn't her steps be light because she was floating on air, such a satisfied customer? Angelo sat up at his desk and ran a hand through his hair.

There was a knock on the door.

'Come in.'

The visitor was Muffin. Her clothes were creased and she looked tired.

On his way back to the stakeout David resolved to bend the truth. A detective was allowed, right? When the situation required it. Like when Dad and Uncle Sal had stopped Mr Shayler on his way home from work.

As it happened Marie was alone when David arrived. She was riffling through a rack of leather jackets that stood on the pavement outside a shop across from the Shaylers. 'I thought you got stuck in the phone box and forgot how to get out again,' she said as her brother arrived.

'Very humorous,' David said. He checked his watch and recorded the time of his return in his notebook. Then he said, 'Dad went on and on, about how it's essential to pay close attention all the time when you're doing surveillance work. And he said he's probably going to check that we're doing it right. If we're not, he won't pay us.'

Marie took a jacket from the rack and held it up for a better look. She knew she was being got at. And it sounded much more like David talking than her father. So she said, 'Well, you better pull your socks up, then.' She tossed her hair.

'Our assessment,' Roger Varden said after ordering, 'is that Adamson was killed by a burglar. We think the burglar was surprised in the act and hit out. Adamson died from a single blow to the head with a blunt object that was not found with the body.'

'A burglar,' Gina repeated. 'Does that mean things were stolen from the house?'

'At least eight old firearms, antiques,' Varden said. 'Half of them pistols. You know, do you, that Adamson had a business repairing antique weapons?'

'I understood he was a printer,' Gina said, 'with the antique weapons more a sideline.'

'He was a printer originally,' Varden said, 'and for most of his working life. But he was made redundant six years ago. With his pay-off he turned a hobby interest in old guns into a business. It was through that connection that he met Cyril Younger.'

'Who is Cyril Younger?'

Varden studied Gina, trying to assess what she did and didn't know, what her agenda was. 'He owns Block Letter.'

'Ah,' Gina said. 'I knew there was an owner. I didn't know his name.'

Varden said, 'Younger's primary business is called Qualico. It imports clothes and trinkets and the like, mostly from Africa. He started it about four years ago. I don't know what his secret is but Qualico is one of those exceptional companies you read about, the ones that grow quickly despite recession.'

'What is Cyril Younger like?'

'He's very smooth – the operator type. And two and a half years ago it seems his Qualico had grown to the point where it paid him to have his own printing set-up.'

'And Cyril Younger is interested in old guns?'

'He bought and sold general antiques as a business before he started Qualico, including antique firearms. There's an antique weapon society in Bath and Younger was active in it. It was through the club that he met Adamson.'

'From whose house eight weapons were stolen. So what was Younger doing on the night of . . .'

'If only police work were so easy, Gina,' Varden said with a laugh. 'Ach, here is my *tortelloni al burro e fromaggio*. Oh yes. That looks wonderful. Perfect.'


'I was wondering,' Muffin began, 'whether maybe Gina was around.'

'I'm sorry,' Angelo said. 'She went out on a job. I don't know when she'll be back.'

Muffin smiled weakly. 'Aren't you guys ever off duty?'

'Nine to five would be a holiday,' Angelo said. 'A vacation, I mean.'

'I thought,' Muffin said, 'I hoped maybe Gina might come out for a walk with me. It's such a nice day.'

'Yes, it is,' Angelo said.

'I could wait,' Muffin said. 'But you don't know when she'll be back?'

'No.'

'Oh.'

'Muffin?' Angelo said.

'Uh huh?'

'You have something on your mind, don't you?'

'I guess I do.'

Angelo said, 'Tell you what. Let's you and me go for a walk. If you feel like talking, fine. If not, then the worst that can happen is that you'll have seen the church Jane Austen's parents were married in. OK?'


'I'm going out,' the Old Man said.

'Oh yes? Where to?'

'A walk.'

'It's a good thing, to move old bones,' Mama said.

'You're coming? Or not?'

'My bones move plenty, thanks. I run around after you, don't I?'

'You don't want to? Don't. I'll run around after myself. Huh!'


'So,' Varden said, 'it's not Cyril Younger you're interested in?'

'No,' Gina said. 'It's the other employee at Block Letter. Howard. I don't know his surname.'

'Well, well,' Varden said. 'Whatever could there be in the life of a nonentity like Howard Urcott that would be of interest to a private detective?'

'If I just told you I wouldn't be wriggling,' Gina said.

Varden savoured a forkful of tortelloni. He wiped his lips with a smile. 'All right,' he said, 'Howard Urcott . . . I found him quiet, shy almost to the point of muteness. He lives with his mother, next door to the murder victim.'

'Is that how he got the job at Block Letter?'

'It is. Mother Urcott – who is probably not mute even when asleep – told me that Adamson was diagnosed with angina about a year ago. He was told to work less so Mother Urcott convinced him to try Howard as a sort of apprentice. Apparently the arrangement worked well enough. Howard began there seven months before Adamson was murdered.'

'Did Howard have a printing background?'

'Howard had no background,' Varden said. 'He'd never had a job before. Can you imagine it, Gina? Twenty-eight years old and never worked.'

'Things are so different for children these days,' Gina said.

'Is that an observation from personal experience?' Varden asked.

'I have two teenagers,' Gina said.

'No!' Varden affected shock.

'Do you have children?'

'No such luck, if luck it be,' Varden said.

'Oh, I think it is,' Gina said, wondering if Varden was married, thinking that to ask on Rosetta's behalf would please Mama.

But Varden said, 'May I ask you a personal question now?'

'All right.'

'When Charlie rang me about you he gave your discretion, scruples, and general worthiness as a receiver of confidences a marvellous reference.'

Gina had been present as Charlie urged Varden to provide whatever information she might wish. She said, 'Did he?'

Varden said, 'I was most impressed that an experienced and highly respected officer like Charlie Stiles would say such things about a private detective, any private detective. Impressed, and curious.'

Gina said, 'My husband's father once solved a problem relating to Charlie's father.'

'And it was sufficiently important for the sense of debt to be passed on through the generations?'

'It was . . . quite a difficult problem,' Gina said.

'I shall have to remember to ask Charlie for details.'

'Meanwhile,' Gina said, 'we were talking about Howard Urcott.'


David spotted Angelo and Muffin walking his way. He was thrilled. Seeing Muffin at all excited him. Seeing her with his father when Marie was trying on a jacket from the rack outside 'Leathers' while at the same time giggling with her two grungy friends was even better. David could have warned Marie of Angelo's approach, but he didn't.

However at the last minute Marie spotted Angelo herself. She immediately left her friends and went to him. 'No action so far, Dad,' she said, as if she had been doing the job properly all along.

There was nothing David could say. Especially not in front of Muffin.

'Stick with it,' Angelo said.

'Nice jacket, Marie,' Muffin said. 'Hi there, Davey.'

'Do you like it?' Marie said. She spun to show the jacket off from all angles.

'Hi,' David said. He wanted to ask Muffin when she was going to come to the house to show him sophisticated tricks on the computer. When she was going to win her bet with Marie. He opened his mouth, but his father spoke first.

'I'll be out of the office for a bit,' Angelo said. 'But ring in anyway. Leave a message on the machine.'

'OK, Dad,' Marie said brightly.

'Back to work now,' Angelo said. He and Muffin walked on.

'Bye, Dad,' David said. 'Bye, Muffin!' Marie returned to her friends.

David looked after Muffin and his father. Then he checked his

125

watch and got out his notebook. '14.36. Dad and Muffin walked by, heading south. Dad says he'll be out for a bit.' He closed his notebook. It was then it hit him. *Muffin!* She left a message last night! I didn't tell anyone. Oh no!

'Howard Urcott was not a happy camper when I interviewed him,' Varden said. 'He was genuinely upset. He assumed that Adamson's death meant he would lose his job. After a taste of employment and independence I don't think he fancied being around his mother's house all the time.'

'You had reason to believe he was involved in the murder, then?'

'To tell you the truth, Gina, it did not cross my mind that he would have it in him. He's a very odd young man, to be sure. But he seemed so meek. He actually cringed whenever I made a quick movement. And there wasn't the slightest suggestion of a motive.'

'He did gain from the killing.'

'That's true, as things have worked out. Do you have some reason to suspect him? Is that what this is about?'

'Not at all,' Gina said. 'I only found out about the murder today. But our case does involve Howard Urcott, and what we are working on doesn't suggest someone silent or meek. More someone socially inept.'

Varden shrugged. 'He did have an alibi of sorts. The Medical Examiner said Adamson was hit in the late evening, but according to Mother Urcott young Howard went to his room at eight and didn't come down again until morning.'

'Eight?' Gina said. 'This boy does make me uneasy.'

'He goes in for video games. They were the first things he bought with his earnings. But Mother Urcott swore most convincingly that if Howard had come down the stairs she would have known, even after she went to bed. It seems that the creaking would inevitably have awakened her.'

'But doesn't Howard's bedroom have a window?' Gina asked.

\*

When Angelo and Muffin had turned a corner, Angelo said, 'Did you notice the two boys?'

'In front of the shop?' Muffin asked. 'Is that who the kids are following?'

'No no,' Angelo said. 'They were talking to Marie. I just wondered if you heard what they said as we went past.'

'I didn't. Sorry,' Muffin said.

'Didn't catch a name? Terry maybe?'


The Old Man stood by the coat cupboard. Should he wear a coat? But it was a sunny day. He went to the door.

'You're *not* going out without your coat, are you?' Mama said.

'Who needs it?' the Old Man said. But he turned back and took his jacket from its hanger. Mama helped him put it on.


'So how was the case left?' Gina asked.

'With no other leads I decided that the only chance was to wait for the antique weapons to turn up. We were fortunate to have photographs and detailed descriptions. If they appear at clubs or specialist dealers anywhere in this country – or Scotland – I'll hear about it.'

'But they haven't appeared.'

'Not so far.'

'And does that surprise you?'

'It does, rather. The weapons are English. Good quality, but not so special as to be of particular interest abroad.'

Gina frowned as she absorbed this information, but her concentration was broken by the arrival of the sweets trolley.

'Gina?' Varden asked.

'Go for the *monte bianco*,' Gina said. 'Then tell me in more detail about the murder scene.'


'I never read Jane Austen,' Muffin said, 'but now I've been here, and seen all these places from her books it's going to be fun.'

'This is Henrietta Park,' Angelo said. 'And down here . . .'

Angelo led her through a wrought-iron gate. 'This little garden was specially planted for its scent.'

'Gosh.'

'Emperor Haile Selassie walked through here every day when he was in exile.'

'An *emperor*?'

'That's right. He was in this country from 1936 to 1941, while we occupied Ethiopia.'

'England occupied Ethiopia?'

'Not England,' Angelo said. 'Italy.'

The policeman had already walked past once before. David had noticed and even considered recording the fact in his notebook. But this time the policeman stopped. 'A word, please, you two.'

'Us?' Marie said.

'That's right. You, and him.'

'What can we do for you, officer?' David said.

'You can tell me what you're up to.'

'We're not up to anything,' Marie said.

'So why have you been hanging around outside this shop since ten this morning?'

'Since 10.31,' David said.

'Why?'

David and Marie looked at each other.

'What's your game?' the policeman said more forcefully.

'Is there some problem, officer?' Marie said sweetly.

'I've had a complaint.'

'But we haven't done anything,' David said.

'So you'll be happy to move along?' the policeman said.

Angelo and Muffin sat on a wooden bench in a bower of roses and honeysuckles.

'Tell me,' Muffin said, 'do you feel more Italian or English?'

'I was born here,' Angelo said. 'I grew up here.'

'Do you speak Italian?'

128

'We used to with Papa, when we were children. But Mama wanted us to speak English. To help her learn, she said.'

'I like your Mama.'

'Me too,' Angelo said.

'Do you go to Italy?'

'Not so often now.'

'But do you like it there?'

'Oh yes.' He smiled. 'Especially the olives.'

'Are they different?'

'Here,' he said, spreading his hands, 'you get one kind or maybe two. There whole stalls in the market offer different olives.'

A duck landed in the rectangular pond at the centre of the garden. Bees buzzed. Butterflies rose and fell.

'This place is *wonderful!*' Muffin said.

'I like it,' Angelo said. 'I come here when I have things to think about. When life seems complicated.'

Muffin nodded, and looked around again. 'I'm so unhappy, Angelo,' she said.

Angelo was taken aback by the direct, personal statement. He was uncertain, even, what she had said.

Muffin said, 'I'm so, so unhappy. I can't get *anything* right. My whole life is a mess.'

'Do you . . . Is it that . . . Would you like to talk about it?'

'I already did. A bit. A tiny bit.'

'Did you?' Angelo said.

'It was at dinner the other night. The first dinner. Oh, that was *so* neat, being there with you guys. You all really have it worked out, don't you?'

'What?'

'Oh, I don't know. Your lives and everything. You all know who you are and what you do. Everybody gets along so well. And you all pull in the same direction, even those great kids of yours. When I think about what I was like at their age . . . Wow, it's a bad memory. But your kids, they already know more about life than I do now. I'm only twenty-seven, but sometimes I wonder how I've screwed up so much in such a short time.'

There was a pause as Angelo tried to work out how he would lead the conversation if he were with a client. He said, 'Are you talking screwed-up professionally, or screwed-up personally?'

'Professionally I'm a star,' Muffin said. 'Personally I'm a fuck-up. Pardon my French. Or I guess maybe I should say my Italian.'

After another moment Angelo said, 'I still don't remember what you told us at dinner.'

'No,' Muffin said. 'And why should you? With all the work you do and all the things you have to think about. It was when we were talking about that dish-washing detergent man. He didn't notice a bottle that was left out. Remember him?'

'I remember him,' Angelo said.

'We were hypothesizing about what could be distracting him. Your dad thought it might be another woman. Do you remember?'

'I remember,' Angelo said.

'Well, I said that it didn't have to be a big thing to distract him. It could be like a girl he started by waving at, only it grew and he could end up by being obsessed with her.'

'And Mama asked if you were talking from personal experience,' Angelo said.

'That's right! Gosh, you *do* remember!'

'You described something from America, from your laboratory. Was it a man who walked past your door who caused you trouble?'

'Sort of,' Muffin said. 'Only it wasn't past the door, and it wasn't the guy. The one who caused the trouble was me.'


'Oh yeah!' the policeman said. 'Pull the other one.'

'We *are* private detectives,' David insisted.

'So where are your magnifying glasses? And you're not carrying a "rod" in that pocket, are you, lad?'

'It's my notebook,' David said.

'It's true, officer,' Marie said. 'We're on a job.'

'What job?' the policeman asked.

David and Marie exchanged glances. David said, 'There are

130

some people we have to follow if they go anywhere. Look at my notebook if you don't believe us.' David opened the notebook and held it out.

With a sigh the policeman looked through David's three pages of surveillance notes. Eventually he said, 'Where does it say who you're watching?'

'I don't think we can tell you that,' David said. 'Can we?' he asked Marie.

'Dad didn't say.'

'Sorry,' David said.

'"Dad didn't say"?' the policeman said. He handed the notebook back. 'Well, *did* Dad say just what he wanted you out of the house for? Because that's what it sounds like to me.'

'It isn't,' David insisted. 'Dad's a private detective too.'

'So why isn't he out here? Or maybe he is.' The policeman looked around. He lifted the arms of one of the leather jackets. 'Come out, come out, wherever you are.'

Anger began to replace David's trepidation. 'You're not taking this seriously!'

'True,' the policeman said. 'And frankly I don't really care if you are playing detectives or not. We've had a complaint. And if you don't want me to take more drastic action, you will move well away from *here*.'

'Who complained?' David asked.

'Sorry,' the policeman said. 'My dad told me not to tell.'

'We need to know,' David insisted. He was fearful that it was the Shaylers.

'Tough,' the policeman said. 'We've had a complaint. I'm checking it out. And as far as I can tell, you two are loitering here with, as they say, intent. You have not explained your continued presence to my satisfaction. If you don't agree to move voluntarily, I will have to take further measures.'

'But that's not fair!' David said.

From behind David a new voice entered the conversation. 'What's the problem here, officer? These two miscreants throwing stones at passing cars, or what?'

David and Marie turned to the new accuser.

'Do you know these young people, sir?' the policeman said.

'I ought to,' the Old Man said. 'I'm their grandfather.'

'Don't tell me,' the policeman said. 'You're a private detective too.'

'I am,' the Old Man said proudly.

With a sigh the policeman said, 'Well then, sir, perhaps you could explain to me why these two youngsters have been standing outside this shop for the past four hours doing nothing except try on jackets and hold conversations with people passing by.'

'Explain?' the Old Man said.

'That's right, sir. Just what are they up to?'

'How should I know?' the Old Man said. 'Nobody tells me anything.'

'Grandad!' Marie said.

'Well, they don't.'

'In that case, sir, perhaps you would assist me in another way, by convincing them to move!'

'Where to?' the Old Man asked.

But Marie tugged at the Old Man's sleeve. 'Grandad. Grandad?'

'Watch the jacket, Marie,' the Old Man said.

'Grandad!' Marie said. 'The Shaylers have just come out of their house!'

# 15

'So,' Charlie said, 'was Roger helpful?'

'Very,' Gina said. 'And his recall of the details of the Adamson case was impressive.'

'He's ambitious,' Charlie said. 'And any unsolved murder case has the potential to advance a career.'

'Well,' Gina said, 'how about your career, Charlie? Are you ambitious?'

Charlie studied her face. 'What are you getting at? What do you know that you didn't tell Varden?'

'It's what he told me.'

'Such as?'

'He says antique firearms were stolen, but nothing else, not even the cash out of Adamson's wallet. A few things like that struck me as odd.'

'Oh,' Charlie said.

'It's probably just that I don't know enough,' Gina said. 'So, I thought you might be able to run me off a copy of everything in the case file. I'll sit in a corner. I'll be invisible.'


'I wouldn't . . . I *couldn't* let Tom alone,' Muffin said. 'I thought about him *all* the time. If I was in the lab, I'd lift things up so an invisible "he" could see what I was doing. If I was working on my thesis, I'd talk to him in my head. I'd say, "Tom, is that a good point, or not?" And of course, I made a nuisance of myself. I'd walk past his apartment again and again. I'd wait outside a movie house or a restaurant if I knew he was going to be there. I called him *all* the time. I'd do anything for a chance to see him. For a chance to get a word with him. For a chance to touch him.'

'And what did he think about this?' Angelo asked.

'He . . . didn't realize how serious it was. At first.'

'Flattered?'

'I guess.'

'Was he responsive?'

Muffin said, 'Responsive-real? Or responsive-in-my-head?' She turned away, but abruptly swung her head back to look into Angelo's eyes. 'Oh he was responsive in the beginning, all right. He was attracted to me. He – what do you say here? Fancied? He "fancied" me. I was young. I was throwing myself at him. I'm pretty. He did what any man would do.'

'Would you say he gave you encouragement?'

'Angelo, honey, if that man inhaled and then looked at me, I'd take the fact he breathed out again as encouragement.'

'But how did it start?'

The question took Muffin into a happier past. 'It started the first time I saw him. He was scolding some students, some other students, really giving them what-for because they'd dropped two soda cans and an empty potato chip bag on the grass in front of the library. He stood there with his hands on his hips, and he made these guys pick the stuff up. And I watched him do it. Then, when they'd put everything in the trash can, Tom turned my way. He didn't know I was there. He didn't know I'd been watching. But as soon as he saw me, this big grin spread all over his face, and I knew that he had been faking the tough stuff with the kids, bluffing them. That if they'd told him to butt out there wouldn't have been a thing he could have done about it. But he had bluffed them and won and it was a feeling he liked. And I knew, right away, that he had won me too.'

'When was that?' Angelo asked.

'Two years, three months and eleven days ago.'

'And when did it end?'

'It didn't,' Muffin said. 'I'm here in Bath, aren't I? Why do you think that happened? Because I followed him here, that's why.'


At the end of the short path that led from their front door to the pavement, the Shaylers turned and walked past the house of their bird-fancying neighbour. They walked slowly. They walked hand-in-hand.

The Old Man, David and Marie left the front of the leather jacket shop with a synchronicity that startled the policeman. As the detection of Lunghis tracked their 'targets', David made entries in his notebook.

The Shaylers waited for a gap in the traffic and then crossed the street. They arrived on the opposite pavement only a few yards in front of where the Lunghi trio now stood.

Each Lunghi was aware of never having met either Shayler face to face. But had the others? And where were the Shaylers headed?

The second question was soon answered. The Shaylers stopped outside the twin doors that led to the Lunghis' home and office. Mrs Shayler tried the handle to the office door.

When she found it locked, she pushed the door bell to the house.


'But where does Salvatore fit in all this?' Angelo asked.

'Don't get me wrong,' Muffin said. 'Sally's a really nice guy. He really is. I like him a lot. And your *family*! I think you guys are about the neatest family I've ever met, I really do.'

'Thank you,' Angelo said.

'When I got to Bath I tracked Tom to the university. And *then* I found out that he's gotten himself a *job* there, and he hadn't even told me! Back in the States when I asked his friends they all said he was going someplace for a couple of weeks' vacation. But when I found out about the job . . . Well, the first thing I thought was how smart I'd been not to stay home. I'd followed him to the airport, see, and then to London and then to Bath. So I guess I'm sort of a private eye myself.'

Angelo nodded.

'But *then* it hit me. How he must have laughed with all his friends about tricking me. And how he obviously meant to get lost and never let me know where he was. Well, I felt so humiliated, so depressed with myself! You just can't imagine.'

Angelo couldn't imagine.

'And *then* I thought to myself, I thought, "Muffin, honey, what *are* you doing?" And it was about the first time I *really* asked myself that, and the answer was that I was peeing my whole life away, because I was dedicating it to someone who didn't give a damn about me, not a single tiny damn. And it was all such a *waste*!'

Carefully Angelo said, 'Had you not come to this assessment before?'

'That's the point, Angelo. I hadn't. Not really. Not so intensely. I mean, I knew before that I'd been stupid. All I had to do was count up everything I did – all the letters, all the calls, drawing his picture over and over, talking to him when he wasn't there, writing him poems. It's *too* embarrassing. Sending him underwear, even. Awful. All I had to do was think about that, and I knew how stupid it all was. But before I got here I'd never *felt* it, not the way I *felt* it last weekend.'

'So, maybe, this trip has been a constructive one for you after all?'

'I sure thought so,' Muffin said. 'I kept saying to myself, "Muffin, honey, you can do *better* than this guy." And that's when I went down to your pub in town and met Salvatore. No, that's wrong. I didn't "meet" him. I picked him up. I can be real predatory when I put my mind to it. I made all the first moves. But don't get me wrong. Salvatore is a real sweetie. I hit lucky there. But then . . .'

'Then?'

'After a couple of days Tom started popping back into my head. And at real intimate times. At first I was able to pop him out of my head again – your brother can be *real* distracting – but Tom kept coming back. I started thinking, "If Tom knew, then he'd be jealous." And I started thinking up ways to let him know. And then last night . . .' Muffin shook her head. 'I was so disgusting. It was like nothing had changed. I didn't care how he had tricked me. I found him up at the university and even though he wouldn't talk to me I followed him home. And I put a lot of notes through the letter slot in his door. And I waited outside.'

'All night?'

'The whole night long,' Muffin said. 'See, I was *sure* he'd realize it was a good thing to have a friend in a strange country. So I just knew that when he thought it through he'd come out. Even if it was only to bring me a blanket. Anything. Something. It would show he still cared.'


'May I help you?' the Old Man said. 'These are my properties.'

'Mr . . . Lunghi?' Jack Shayler said.

'That's me.'

Shayler glanced at his wife and said, 'My name is Shayler. Eileen, my wife, tells me that she consulted you recently.'

Mrs Shayler took her husband's elbow and drew close to him.

'Ah,' the Old Man said. 'Not me personal, but junior members of my staff.'

'Well, Mr Lunghi, Eileen and I have talked things over and we've decided to ask for some advice. It's about the rather worrying situation that started this whole business.'

'Advice, we specialize in,' the Old Man said.

'We know it's short notice, but we're prepared to pay a premium if you can arrange for a prompt consultation.'

The Old Man said, 'Normally, a Saturday, we don't work. But we can make an exception.'

'Thank you, Mr Lunghi,' Jack Shayler said. 'We're very grateful, aren't we, Eileen?'

With a beatific smile, Mrs Shayler said, 'Oh yes. Thank you.'

'One minute,' the Old Man said, holding up a finger. He turned to David and Marie. 'The job, I think, is finished, yes? Later your father will pay but I give you money too.' He took out his wallet. 'Get a decent lunch, have a little fun. Be back . . .' He looked at his watch. '5.30.' He gave each grandchild a ten-pound note.

Marie could hardly believe her luck.

David could hardly believe that he was not to be allowed to continue just when things were about to get interesting. After all those hours standing and watching the house!

The Old Man turned back to the Shaylers. 'Now we go up to my flat and consult. Let my wife make tea. See if we can give some satisfaction.'


'Muffin,' Angelo said, 'why did you ring Gina last night?'

'I'm embarrassed to say now,' Muffin said, 'I was so cold and so crazy! But I thought maybe I could hire your agency.'

'Hire us? To do what?'

'To follow Tom for me. To make reports. And, maybe . . .'

'What?'

'Well, Salvatore told me how you and he scared that poor dish-washing detergent guy. Well, I thought maybe you could do something to . . . to scare Tom. Some last-ditch thing to

137

make him realize that he should make his life with me and not
. . . somebody else. Maybe . . .' She lowered her eyes, 'Maybe
hurt him.'

Angelo stiffened. 'We couldn't! We don't!'

Muffin covered her face. 'I know. I know. But, please, Angelo
. . . Even when I'm thinking straight these days I'm thinking
crooked.'

They sat in silence for a few moments. Then Angelo said,
'Muffin, I think it's time for you to look at the larger picture.'

'What do you mean?'

'For a while, last weekend, you were thinking straight.'

'I guess,' Muffin said.

'On a hard detective case a little progress sometimes, that's
success,' Angelo said. 'You shouldn't forget a step forward even
if later you take half a step back. Papa says that.'

'He's a pretty smart old guy, your dad,' Muffin said.

'Yeah,' Angelo said. 'He is.'

'But it still doesn't answer the question,' Muffin said. 'What
do I do *now*?'

'You should talk to someone.'

'I am. I'm talking to you.'

'But you should talk to someone who can help.'

'You *are* helping.'

'I mean . . .'

'I know what you mean,' Muffin said. 'You mean a professional, a therapist.'

'Well . . .'

'I know. I know, I know, I know. But it's so shaming. So
humiliating! It'd be like a confession.'

'But,' Angelo said, 'you confessed to me.'

'And telling you wasn't humiliating at all.'

'Think it through. You feel bad. All right, what would make
you feel better?'

'Angelo,' Muffin said, 'you're so sweet to listen to me talk. I
must seem a real nutcase.'

'No, no, no,' Angelo said.

'But I *am* grateful. I really am. And I do know what would

make me feel better. A *whole* lot better. But . . . it's not something I can do alone.'


Mama was on the telephone with her friend, Gabriella, from the same Piedmontese village as Mama and the Old Man. Gabriella was planning her youngest daughter's wedding. The celebration was getting bigger every day, which made for many problems.

Mama had sympathy for Gabriella's plight. She contributed to the talk about wedding plans with enthusiasm. And if the event's approach made it easy for Mama to continue to omit the news about Walter's absence, so much the better. Perhaps Walter would be back – or replaced – by the time the wedding was successfully executed. Or, God forbid, cancelled.

Then Mama heard footsteps. She said, 'Oh, *he's* on the stairs.' Gabriella understood immediately, and said goodbye. Mama hung up the telephone and picked up a duster. She was facing the door when her husband walked in.

'Back already from your walk?' Mama asked. 'No stamina?'

Mama was not surprised when the Old Man did not answer her. But she was surprised when a man in his mid-forties and a woman in her mid-thirties followed the Old Man through the door. And she was astonished when he introduced them as Mr and Mrs Shayler.


'Do you want some of my fries?' David asked.

'Your yukky fries with mustard all over them?'

'*And* blue cheese mayonnaise off the burger,' David said. 'Good. Good. Good.'

'No, I do not want any of your fries,' Marie said.

'What are you going to do now?' David asked.

Marie considered. 'I'll think of something.'

'Shouldn't we look for Dad?'

'Why?'

'To see if we're really finished with the job.'

'Grandad said we were. So we are.'

'I know,' David said, 'but – '

'What I say don't count around here all of a sudden?' Marie said in a deepened voice and with intonations that David recognized immediately.

David giggled at the accuracy of voice and content. Marie laughed too and said, 'Careful, you'll spill your shake.' She tossed her hair.

'My shake don't count around here all of a sudden?' David mimicked.

'You're not half as good at him as I am,' Marie said.

David agreed by not contradicting. 'But really, shouldn't we look for Dad? He'd want to know, wouldn't he? We've got to report.'

Marie considered. They could charge it as more working time. Why not? 'Where?'

'Well, he's with that Muffin,' David said as casually as he could.

'*Doctor* Muffin to you,' Marie said.

'He's probably showing her tourist things. We could try the Abbey and the Roman Baths.'

Marie straightened, struck by an idea.

'Marie?' David said.

'Yeah, all right,' Marie said with mysterious resolution. 'Let's look for Dad and Doc Muffin down the Abbey. Come on, *Davey*.'


'Charlie,' Gina said, 'is this all there is on the Adamson case?' She held up the computer print-out she had been studying.

'Don't even ask,' Charlie said. 'I don't have access, and what you've seen already would get me sacked.'

'I understand,' Gina said, holding her hands up.

Charlie thought about it. 'You could talk to Varden again.'

'He won't be back till later,' Gina said.

'Will I regret it if I ask?'

Gina tried to explain her unease. 'You've got a burglary in a modest house. The burglar is surprised by the homeowner, so

140

the burglar whacks the homeowner on the head. And it all takes place about midnight.'

'OK,' Charlie said.

Gina said, 'After the burglar hits the homeowner, he leaves the house, but he doesn't go empty-handed. He takes eight antique pistols and rifles. So he hasn't panicked.'

'Sounds reasonable.'

'But the first thing I don't understand,' Gina said, 'is that there is nothing in what I've read that mentions a forced entry.'

Charlie shrugged. 'So maybe entry wasn't forced.'

'Maybe,' Gina said. 'But the house was pretty secure, in line with standards set by the antique gun club. To me that suggests a professional burglar.'

'OK,' Charlie said. 'A professional.'

'But all he took were the weapons. And they are relatively difficult to sell. Why nothing else?'

'Well . . .' Charlie's face suggested that he took the point, but did not think it conclusive.

'And he left cash. Thirty-eight pounds in Adamson's wallet. Why would a pro do that, Charlie?'

'Didn't want to hang around a dead body?'

'The body wasn't dead. The ME's report said Adamson took hours to die. So was it a pro, or an amateur?'

'Sorry,' Charlie said. 'I'm just a poor computer copper. You're the private eye.'

'Of course,' Gina said, 'all this is probably resolved in the full case file.'

'You got a problem,' the Old Man said when the Shaylers were settled on the couch. 'We'll talk about that in a moment, but so everybody knows what's what, we better agree money.'

'I appreciate your direct manner, Mr Lunghi,' Jack Shayler said.

'Suppose we go fixed-fee and then just let it take whatever time it takes,' the Old Man said. He suggested a figure. 'That's acceptable?'

'In the circumstances, very acceptable,' Jack Shayler said. 'Eileen?'

Mrs Shayler took a cheque book from her handbag and passed it to her husband. Jack Shayler wrote a cheque and passed it to the Old Man who examined it and then put it in a pocket. At that moment, Mama appeared with a tray.

The Old Man said, 'Tea we throw in free.'


David and Marie approached the Abbey from the Guildhall side, but long before they got there the density of the town-centre crowds was evident. The pavements were packed and currents of people passed in and out of the shop-lined passageways. The quantity of humanity did not please Marie. 'Bloody tourists,' she said.

'If it's so crowded here, maybe they went to the Parade Gardens,' David said, looking across the traffic circle to the park beside the river.

'Go and look there if you like,' Marie said. She continued toward the Abbey.

After an indecisive moment David followed his sister. 'It's getting on for teatime,' he said. 'Maybe you're right. Maybe he took her to the Pump Room.'


Getting out of the Ham Gardens car-park proved a great deal easier than getting into it. That was just as well because Gina was preoccupied with what she had read in Charlie's room. And there would be more to come if Charlie could manage to catch Varden.

At Henry Street Gina turned right, and got hooted at because she hadn't realized quite how close the oncoming car was. She waved to acknowledge her error, but the other driver hooted at her again. He's probably tired after a long day shopping, Gina thought.

Although Gina's day had been long, she was not tired. She was excited. But she recognized that even for the short drive to home she would have to buck up her concentration on the external world. She moved early into the left-hand lane for a turn at the corner.

Traffic slowed Gina's progress to the lights at the foot of North Parade. But no sooner had she crossed the intersection and turned into the Orange Grove roundabout than she saw David and Marie crossing to the Abbey courtyard. Impulsively, Gina hooted at them. Neither of her children noticed. But the driver of the car in front of her did. He turned and waved a fist.

Gina ignored him. She was puzzled why the children should be heading that way, at this time of day, together.

The car behind Gina hooted, and she moved ahead until she was stopped again, at the next lights. Then Gina remembered that David and Marie were working, following the Shaylers. If David and Marie were together, then the Shaylers were together. Gina smiled. Chances were that Angelo was paying the children to follow the Shaylers as they went into town to do their shopping.

Gina's smile evaporated a few hundred yards closer to home. As she waited by the Pig and Fiddle to turn into Walcot Street, a glance to the right confirmed that there was no oncoming traffic. But the same glance caught sight of Muffin and Angelo across the road. Muffin and Angelo were together. They were holding hands. And they were headed for the entrance of the Hilton Hotel.

# 16

The longer he trailed after Marie the more convinced David became that she was not looking for their father. Marie seemed, instead, to be checking out the buskers along Stall Street, especially those with big crowds around them.

At first David thought Marie had decided their father would be showing Muffin Bath's buskers. Maybe they didn't have buskers in America. But it soon became obvious that Marie was not studying the crowds, she was studying the buskers themselves. She would push to the front but once there she retreated and refused to stop and watch.

David enjoyed Bath's buskers. On an ordinary Saturday he might well walk into town and spend his time going from one street act to the next. They came from miles around to perform in Bath, especially in good weather, and especially on Saturdays.

Marie's rapid retreats offended David. He felt it was only courtesy to spend at least a couple of minutes watching or listening. It was also courteous to give money. It wasn't as if he and Marie didn't have any. There was plenty of change from the Old Man's tenners. Plus whatever their father paid them later. Marie was just so tight-fisted. Chronic, in fact. Nevertheless David continued to follow his sister while keeping his eyes peeled for his father and Muffin.

Eventually Marie led away from the Abbey and into the small square called Abbey Gardens. Here there was a juggling clown, and at the far side a musical group. Marie ignored the clown entirely and made for the thin crowd listening to the musicians.

When David caught up she said, 'How do you like these?'

'Which?'

'This group, thickness!'

David looked at the three young men. One played a keyboard. One played a wailing clarinet. A third sang into a microphone that, along with the keyboard, was powered by a car battery. The music owed a lot to reggae and was not jazzy enough to suit David's taste. 'They're OK,' he said.

'Shows what you know!' Marie said.

Because the amplification was not of very good quality David could hear only snatches of the lyric. 'Lit-tle girl,' the singer sang. 'Lit-tle vir-gin and ton-ic.'

'Do you like them?' David asked.

'I think they sound mega,' Marie said without evident pleasure. 'But I think they would do a lot lot better financially if they had a girl dancer.'

David looked at the buskers again. 'You really think that would help?' he said.

'A girl dancer in a short skirt,' Marie said. 'She could be a backing singer on some of the numbers. And during the others

144

she could go around the crowd collecting with a hat. I think it would make *all* the difference.'

Jack Shayler said, 'This is all very hard for me to talk about, Mr Lunghi. As my poor wife has already found.' He patted Eileen Shayler's arm.

The Old Man said, 'In your own time.'

'You already know, I expect, that I work for a firm of accountants, Whitfield, Hare and O'Shea.'

The Old Man nodded.

'Although I am only a clerk there, I've been happy enough. Eileen and I have modest needs and I have the satisfaction of knowing that I do good work. The youngsters who come into the firm these days may cut corners but I always say that there is nothing like detail and routine to ensure quality work. I always say that, don't I, dear?'

'You certainly do, dear,' Mrs Shayler said with approval.

'My job involves examining the financial records that a client submits. I check the maths, and I look at the supporting receipts and invoices to make sure everything's been dealt with properly. I'm not claiming,' Jack Shayler said, 'that I validate every piece of paper which crosses my desk. But, if I do say so myself, I am the one clerk in the firm who always stands ready to go that extra mile. Or perhaps I should say "that extra kilometre", in these days of such close association with our European neighbours.' Shayler paused, smiling at his own joke.

Mrs Shayler smiled. Mama nodded. The Old Man said, 'Go on.'

'One of the ways I go the extra kilometre is to help out when colleagues are ill or away. So when young Francis came down with gastroenteritis I went to his in-tray and picked up the file for a client called Qualico and began to work on it. Qualico is a Bath firm that imports goods for resale, mostly from African manufacturers. It's run by a man called Cyril Younger who is a friend of one of our partners, Mr Guy English. Mr English always works on Mr Younger's accounts himself, but he does sometimes let new clerks check the figures. That way he can see

145

for himself whether they are picking up errors the way they should.'

'So this Francis is a new clerk,' the Old Man said, 'but ill. And you found something disturbing in the Qualico?'

'Exactly,' Jack Shayler said. 'You have gone straight to the nub, Mr Lunghi. Eileen said you people were good, and you have fully justified her evaluation.'

The Shaylers exchanged smiles.

Mama said, 'So what was the problem?'

'Shush,' the Old Man said. 'The man is telling.'

'The receipt in question,' Jack Shayler said, 'the *first* receipt in question, was for the purchase of a large quantity of drums with hollowed-log bases and water buffalo hide tops. The purchase was made by a Qualico agent in Malawi. It was one of many large purchases made in Africa, leading to the accumulation there of nearly three million pounds' worth of stock, at import value.'

'Sounds like a lot of drums,' the Old Man said.

'Indeed,' Jack Shayler said. 'So imagine my surprise when I discovered a secondary impression on the back of the receipt that read, "Printed by Block Letter, Bath."'


Once the car was locked in the garage, Gina went to the office. She was not surprised to find it empty, but she had hoped to find a note from Angelo. Perhaps there was one in the house. But before she crossed to look, she went to the answering machine which showed that there were two messages.

The first was nothing, a silent pause.

The second message was, indeed, from Angelo. His voice was breathy. He said, 'I'll be back late.'

That was it? No explanation? No nothing?


After her lunch Rosetta was full of the joys of early summer. It was a beautiful day and she was in no hurry to get back home. Some shopping? Maybe. But she felt a genuine pleasure in being out, of participating in the great tide of humanity, at not being just something washed up on the shore.

She wandered the colonnaded pedestrian thoroughfares in the heart of the city and discovered that she did not want to leave the glory of the day for the darkness of a shop. Instead she stopped to look at the wares on sale from street stalls: jewellery, candles . . . It was good, this life. Better than she had ever realized. He likes me, she thought. He *likes* me. He likes *me*!

'Auntie Rose?'

Rosetta looked to the voice and found Marie, with David not far behind. 'Hello!' She went to them and gathered both in her arms. 'Isn't it a beautiful day!'

David and Marie were surprised by their aunt's enthusiasm and display of affection. Marie worked it out first. 'How was lunch?' she said. 'How did it go?'

'Oh, all right, I suppose,' Rosetta said, affecting calm. She did not affect it well. Her face broke into a huge smile.

'Auntie Rose!' Marie said. The two women grabbed each others' arms and danced up and down on the spot.

David looked on, in some puzzlement.

'Tell me!' Marie said. 'Tell me all about it.'

'Oh, not here,' Rosetta said. 'Where are you going now?'

'Oooh!' Marie said, suffering the pain caused by the conflict between desire and duty. 'Oooh! We promised we'd be home by 5.30.'

'I'm not ready to go home yet,' Rosetta said. 'La-la-la,' she sang, and she spun around.

'Oooh!' Marie said, knowing that denial of duty meant risking her money. 'But we're still on for tonight, aren't we, Auntie Rose? You're still coming out, aren't you? Or are you otherwise engaged?'

'I'm not engaged,' Rosetta said. 'Not yet. But he's coming to lunch tomorrow!'

'Auntie Rose!' Marie said, and the two women danced again.

When they separated Rosetta asked, 'What time tonight? Eight?'

'Seven?' Marie said.

'All right,' Rosetta said. She began to move on.

'I can't *wait!*' Marie said.

David said, 'Auntie Rose, you haven't seen Dad or Muffin, have you?'

The house was as empty as the office. While that was not unusual on a Saturday afternoon, Gina found it seriously frustrating. There were things to do, and things she wanted to talk about.

Gina sat at the kitchen table. She considered making a cup of tea. But she felt too impatient for tea. She considered beginning preparations for the evening meal. The things were in the fridge. But she didn't feel like getting them out.

The telephone rang. Ah, she thought, now he has more time, he's rung back. 'Gina Lunghi.'

Gina heard someone swallow at the other end of the line. Then a man said, 'Hello, Gina. Is Rosetta there, please?'

After a pause for recognition Gina said, 'Walter?'

'That's right.'

'Where are you?'

'At my office.'

'In Bath?'

'Of course. What other office would it be? Oh, excuse me, Gina. I didn't mean to be snappish. It's just, well, I'm a little nervous.'

'I thought . . .' Gina began. 'I didn't think Rosetta was expecting to hear from you.'

'I managed to get back from my trip early. I came into the office to catch up on correspondence. And while I was here I thought I'd ring Rose.'

'I'm afraid she's out.'

'Oh.'

'Do you want to leave a message?'

Walter hesitated. 'Gina, how much has she told you?'

Only that you had a vasectomy without telling her and then went off on holiday with your wife. 'Not much,' Gina said.

'Well, I will leave a message. And it's important. But it may not make much sense to you.'


'Have you done much modelling?' Salvatore asked.

'Oh, a lot. Just never like this before. Some of my friends who are models have, but I haven't.'

'Well, you've got very good bone structure,' Salvatore said. 'In fact very good structure altogether.'

'Thanks. Am I staying still enough?'

'You're doing fine,' Salvatore said. 'I'd never be able to tell it was your first time.'

'It's funny, I feel perfectly comfortable.'

'I'm pleased about that,' Salvatore said. 'But to be on the safe side, I'll mark you in with charcoal.'

'You'll do what?'

'I'll make the marks on the cloth so you can get back into the right position if you want to stretch. Or whatever.'


The last thing Gina wanted to think about was Walter's personal life. And you don't get much more personal than that. She wrote his message on a piece of paper. Then she folded it and wrote Rosetta's name on the outside. But instead of leaving it in the plastic tray on the kitchen table, Gina went to Rosetta's room and slipped the note beneath the door. Not that anybody else would look at it, but it didn't seem quite the thing for Rosetta to read in public.

Gina looked at her watch. Rose must be having a good time. Well, she deserved some luck.

Then Gina contemplated the possible nature of Rosetta's luck. Impulsively, she bolted down the stairs.


'So what did you do?' the Old Man asked.

'The only thing I could,' Jack Shayler said. 'I took the receipt to my boss, Mr English.'

'And he said what?'

Jack Shayler's face showed that it wasn't a pleasant memory. 'He said I should never have touched the file in the first place. He'd left it for Francis because he wanted Francis to work on it. He told me to forget about whatever I thought I'd found. He told me there was no problem. He told me to bring him all the Qualico accounts immediately. And, he used coarse language.'

Eileen Shayler clung to her husband's arm.

'I . . .' Jack Shayler said, 'I'm not used to being spoken to that way.'

'What did you do?' the Old Man asked.

'I took the file to Mr English.'

Mrs Shayler said, 'My Jack didn't tell me what happened so as not to upset me.'

'But I couldn't forget it,' Jack Shayler said. 'I couldn't ignore it. Not something like that. If there's a query about a receipt it must be resolved. That's basic. A matter of professional integrity. A matter of honour. No, I couldn't ignore it.'

'But a difficult situation,' the Old Man said. 'I can see.'

'So before I returned the file I copied the telephone number of the purchasing agent in Malawi. If the agent confirmed that he had his forms printed here in Bath that would explain it.'

'You rang?' the Old Man said.

'Yes. But I couldn't do it from work, so I used the telephone box. Or, at night, the telephone at home.'

'And?'

'There is no such number in Malawi.'

'Huh!' the Old Man said. 'Millions of pounds, but no phone. Huh!'

'My only other available course of action was to ring Block Letter. But as I could only ring out of business hours, the person there turned out to be difficult to contact. So I wrote a letter, giving the number at the telephone box and the exact times for the person to ring me back. When that didn't happen, I wrote again asking that he write to me at work. But there was no response.'

'So he worried,' Mrs Shayler said.

'So I worried,' Jack Shayler said. 'Because Mr English had seemed so angry. He was almost . . . violent.'

Mrs Shayler patted her husband's hand.

'And then,' Jack Shayler said, 'I wrote a final note saying if he didn't ring back I'd be forced to go to the police. It was sheer bluster, of course, but in accountancy one has to be up to that sort of thing now and again.'

When David and Marie got home there was no one in the house. 'Do you think we should go to Grandad's flat?' David asked his sister.

'Why?' Marie said. 'It's not him we're working for.'

'Don't you want to know what happened with the Shaylers?'

'Of course I do,' Marie said, 'but Auntie Rose is more exciting. I can't wait to hear what happened at lunch!'

'Why is that more exciting than the Shaylers?'

'You have no soul,' Marie said. 'There's no love in you. You're just a *thing*.'

'No, I'm not.'

'Oh yes, you are!' Marie flounced to her bedroom.

David didn't quite know what to do with himself. He took an apple from the fruit bowl on the dresser. Then he went to the foot of the stairs that led to his grandparents' flat.

But people never went up uninvited. David didn't know why, but he knew it wasn't done. Much as he wanted to go up, he knew he mustn't.

So he crossed to the office. There he gathered his cartoons. What he had in mind was to begin the process of transferring them into the computer.

But as he held the drawings he found that they pleased him. He smiled, even laughed aloud. Which was not to say that they couldn't be improved if he drew them again.

Instead of moving to the computer David got some clean sheets of paper. He began to draw. And he began to get ideas for new cartoons. Not on the subject of legal practitioners this time, but on buskers!

*

Marie rang Jenny from her room to say she would be at the bus station by 7.15.

'Is *Terry* coming?' Jenny asked.

'Nooo!' Marie said. 'Don't be mean. But I am bringing my Auntie Rose.'

'You're doing *what*?'

'It's OK,' Marie said. 'I know she's old, but she's just like a person really. And, she's in love!'

'She can give you some tips then,' Jenny said.

'Stop it!'

'Well, come on, Marie! Did you go to *see* him?'

'I found the time to drift past with my little brother.'

'And were there a lot of people?'

'Hardly any!' Marie said. 'It was *wonderful*!'


Mama and the Old Man both saw the Shaylers to the door. Then they returned to the kitchen, but found no signs that anybody was about. 'We leave a note, I think,' Mama said.

'Why?' the Old Man said.

'Angelo and Gina might worry.'

'Worry? Suddenly we're not grown up? We're out late, it will make us fall asleep at school tomorrow?'

'Well . . .' Mama said.

'I'm ringing the taxi. You can come. You can stay. Me, I'm on my way.'


When the telephone rang Salvatore was in two minds about answering it. But he rolled over and picked up the receiver by the bed. 'Yo.'

'It's Gina.'

'Hey, Gina,' he said lazily. 'You decided to give up that no account brother of mine at last?'

'Sally,' Gina said, 'is Muffin there?'

'Not unless she's hiding somewhere.'

'Have you talked to her today?'

'Not a word.'

'What hotel was she staying at?'

'The Hilton.'

'And what's her surname?'

'Meckel. And she takes size five shoes. And she has unusually long little fingers. And she never eats rhubarb. Why all the questions, sis?'

'I'm just trying to track her down,' Gina said.

'You sound like a big game hunter.'

Gina hesitated. 'She promised to show David some tricks on the computer. I want to arrange a time.'

'Well, let me know what arrangement you make,' Salvatore said, 'because I've "tracked down" a great new model and I'm thinking of displaying her head at lunch tomorrow.' Salvatore turned to the head on the other pillow and winked. 'She's got great bone structure.'

'The pips are about to go,' Gina said. 'Thanks for the help.'

'Any time,' Salvatore said and they both hung up. Then he turned to his model. 'What do you say?'

'About what?'

'Lunch tomorrow with my family.'

'Really?' But before Salvatore could respond, she said, 'Oh no. I can't. I'm working lunchtime.'

'Another day then, maybe,' Salvatore said.

'Sal?'

'What?'

'Are you disappointed that it's me modelling and not Kit?'

'Certainly not.'

'Really?'

'To tell you the truth,' Salvatore said, 'when I came into the Rose and Crown and asked you for her phone number, it was only an excuse to ask you.'

'Really?' Cheryl said.

'Really,' Salvatore said.

But he paused before returning to his endeavours. What was Gina doing ringing about David and his computer from a public telephone?

*

When Rosetta finally decided to come home it was with hopes of being able to tell Gina all about her lunch before going out and telling Marie all about her lunch. However Gina was nowhere to be found.

But Rosetta was not in a mood to sustain disappointment. She decided to wash and change, and then see if Marie wanted to leave early. Why wait? Rosetta went to her room. Just inside, on the floor, she found the folded paper that Gina had left. Humming to herself, Rosetta opened the message from Walter.


Gina put her last coin in the telephone at the Hilton. She rang the police station and asked for Charlie. It took so long for the switchboard to put her through that Gina began to worry that she'd have to get more change and ring back. But at last Charlie came on the line. 'I have a bone to pick with you, Gina Lunghi,' he said. 'Because of you I'm doing unpaid overtime now.'

'Was Varden helpful? Did you get a look at the Adamson file?'

'He was and I did,' Charlie said.

'And?'

'Even as we speak Varden is out looking for Howard Urcott. He thinks Urcott may well have beaten Adamson to death. Can you come to the station? I'll go through it for you. Briefly.'

'I'll be right over,' Gina said.

After she hung up, Gina turned and caught sight of the hotel's reception desk. If she hadn't agreed to meet Charlie immediately, would she have gone to the desk and asked for Muffin Meckel's room number?

No. I'm too mature to do something like that, Gina decided as she walked out the door.

But if that's the truth, she asked herself as she walked past the Podium, what was I doing in the Hilton in the first place?


Rosetta's door was ajar but Marie knocked on it anyway. She said, 'Auntie Rose, it's seven.'

'Is it?' Rosetta sat on the edge of her bed supporting her head with her hands.

'Is something wrong?'

Rosetta sighed and rose. 'Nothing's wrong. I was just hoping your mother would come home. Do you know where she is?'

'No. Sorry,' Marie said.

'Or how long she'll be?'

'I haven't seen her since this morning.'

'Never mind,' Rosetta said.


Mama and the Old Man stood in front of Block Letter. 'So now you've seen it,' Mama said. 'Are you happy? Have you learned something?'

The Old Man shook the door. It was locked, but loose enough to rattle.

Mama said, 'You expected him to be open for business?'

'His kind of funny business,' the Old Man said, 'who can tell?'

'And if you found him, then what? He would have confessed to something?'

The Old Man pushed hard against the door. It didn't give.

'What are you doing?' Mama asked.

'What does it look?' The Old Man pushed the door again, unsuccessfully. He stepped back.

'Stop being silly!' Mama said.

'Huh!' the Old Man said. Lowering his shoulder he stepped hard toward the door. Wood in the frame splintered. The door flew open. The Old Man fell forward, but maintained his balance. He turned to Mama. 'You're staying outside? To direct traffic?'

Mama examined the door frame's damage. 'I hope you're pleased with yourself.'

The Old Man was extremely pleased with himself. 'I'm closing the door,' he said. 'Are you in or out?'

Mama entered Block Letter.

'Close it behind,' the Old Man said.

'I'm supposed to fix it? Where's the hammer and nails?'

'So lean, if it won't stay shut.'

Mama looked around. She found a cardboard box and pulled

it over to hold the door shut. Then she found a light switch and threw it. Two fluorescent bulbs flickered into life overhead. 'We're going to gaol anyway,' she said, 'so do you want to tell me what's so important to look for?'


When Gina returned home she went straight to the office in case Angelo had left a message. She found David crouched on the floor, drawing. She stood for a minute and watched him work. 'David?'

'Oh, hi, Mum,' David said after a quick glance.

'Have you heard from your father?' Gina said.

'Not since this afternoon. He was with Muffin.'

'Did he say where they were going?'

'No.'

'And he hasn't called in the last hour or so?'

'No.'

'Have you eaten?'

'No,' David said.

'Are you hungry?'

'No.'

Gina felt frustration at the one-sidedness of the conversation. Especially because there were things to say, things to talk to Angelo about. She said, 'I've been at the police station with Charlie.'

David continued drawing.

'Aren't you interested?' Gina said.

After a pause, without looking up, David said, 'Sure, Mum. But I'm finishing something.'

'Well,' Gina said, 'I'm going to get something to eat. If you get it done, or if you get hungry, you can come across and I'll explain to you why the police are out looking for Howard right now, and why they think he may be a murderer.'

# 17

As Mama and the Old Man made their way through Block Letter's files, they discovered business stationery printed with an enormous variety of African company names and addresses.

'They got no printers in Africa? They have to print such things in Bath?' the Old Man said. 'Huh!'

Despite herself, Mama was impressed that their illicit entry had borne such obvious fruit. 'So what do we do?' she asked. 'Put it back where we found it?'

'One each,' the Old Man said.

'What?'

'We take samples, like blood. One each. Make a pile.'

They made a pile. There were many files to sample. The pile grew rapidly.

Then they heard voices, outside. Two men were talking and they seemed to be near the Block Letter door. The sounds froze both Mama and the Old Man while at the same time melting each inside.

When the voices stopped the Old Man moved a finger to his lips, signalling Mama not to make any noise. As if she needed to be told *that*.

But nothing happened. Nobody knocked or tried to enter. Mama looked to the Old Man. He shrugged. Mama eased herself to the plastic window. She could see no one. She turned back to the Old Man and shook her head.

'Back to work,' he said.


Jenny was at the bus station when Marie and Rosetta arrived. Marie introduced her aunt and then asked, 'Well, where shall we go?'

'I talked to Olive,' Jenny said, 'and she says they're definitely not serving without IDs at the Cat and Fountain.'

'Their loss,' Marie said, and she tossed her hair.

Jenny said, 'So what I thought was, since we're at the bus station anyway, why don't we all go up to the university. We'll make the fare back because drinks at the Union are cheap.' Jenny suddenly looked at Rosetta. She put her hand over her mouth and made an have-I-made-an-oopsie? face.

'It's OK,' Marie said. 'Auntie Rose knows I drink, don't you, Auntie Rose?'

Rosetta did now. She nodded.

'Great!' Jenny said. 'So you can go to the bar for us even if they get fusspotty about IDs up there.'

The prospect of going somewhere, of being with people who were lighthearted, drew Rosetta back toward the lightness she'd enjoyed all afternoon. The lightness that had been so abruptly snuffed by the message from Walter. Forget Walter. Rosetta said, 'I don't know whether I've got *my* ID with me, but who needs it?' She pulled her full skirt well up above her knees and waved one leg about cancan-like.

'Great!' Jenny said, and the three women headed toward the university bus stop with arms around each others' waists.


Gina sat at the kitchen table. She was chewing on a piece of cold chicken when David came in.

'Mum?'

'Yes?'

'What was that about murder?'

'There's more chicken in the fridge if you want some,' Gina said.

'You said about Howard being a murderer.'

'If you don't want chicken, I think there's some ham left.'

'*Mum!*' David said.

Gina looked up smiling. 'I spent most of the afternoon talking to policemen who think that Howard may have beaten an old man to death!'


The pile of African business stationery samples was nearly an inch thick when Mama and the Old Man heard a motor vehicle.

It stopped outside Block Letter. Then Mama and the Old Man heard vehicle doors slam.

Before either could say anything, someone crashed into the Block Letter door and it clattered open. The cardboard box put up only token resistance.

Two young men rushed in. The first saw the Old Man. 'There's someone in here!' he said.

As the second turned to pull the door shut he saw Mama by the window. 'Here's another one! We've caught ourselves a couple of fucking thieves.'

Although there was no one else on the bus as it climbed the hill to the university, the three women squeezed on to a single seat. Marie said, 'Let's do lies!'

'Good plan!' Jenny said.

'I don't understand,' Rosetta said.

'What we do,' Marie said, 'is we think up one lie for each of us to tell about ourselves and we stick to them all evening. It's mega.'

'What kind of lie?' Rosetta asked.

'What did we use that time?' Jenny asked.

'Like one time Jenny said she was Mick Jagger's god-daughter,' Marie said.

'Oh, that's right!' Jenny said. 'And this dozy pillock asked me if I still got birthday presents from him! Remember?'

'All black leather and pimples. Yuk!' Marie said. 'And another time I said I worked at a kennel as a dog-mater. And I told them all about how I got the dogs to do it.' The two younger women flooded the bus with laughter.

Then Jenny said, 'Right, what lies shall we do tonight?'

Faced with angry young men who had caught her in an act of blatant illegality, Mama had no words. She could only cross herself between involuntarily deep breaths.

However the Old Man stepped forward. He pointed a finger at the young man who was closer to him. 'You tell me now,' he said. 'Which one of you is this Howard who pretends to be a private detective?'


Although there were no signs indicating the way to the Student Union bar, Jenny and Marie led Rosetta up the stairs and through the boxy corridors without error or hesitation. 'Years of practice,' Marie said.

The bar itself was almost empty. A few drinkers, all male, were scattered around the large scruffy room. One sat on a stool talking to the barman. The three women settled in a cluster of vinyl-covered chairs.

Rosetta volunteered to buy the first round of drinks.

'See?' Marie said to Jenny. 'I knew it was a good idea to ask her along.' Jenny requested a large rum and coke. Marie decided that sounded good too.

When the barman turned from the drinker on the stool to ask Rosetta what she wanted, Rosetta ordered three large rum and cokes. Well, why not?

The man on the bar stool said, 'All for you?'

'No, I'm with friends,' Rosetta said. Then she was disappointed she hadn't thought of something snappier.

The man was rather good-looking in an academic way. He wore glasses and a Greenpeace T-shirt. He sat beside a half-empty pint of stout. 'Hi,' he said. 'I haven't seen you in here before.'

'I haven't been in here before,' Rosetta said.

'Celebrating the end of exams?'

'No. I'm just visiting. I'm a nurse.' Her lie.

'Interesting,' the man said. 'How do you do. My name's Bernard.'


'I'm really glad you came,' Muffin said.

'Me too,' Angelo said.

'Explain it all to Salvatore for me, will you?'

'I will,' Angelo said.

'You really are a lovely man, Angelo Lunghi.' Muffin kissed

him full on the mouth and held him close. 'Thank you. I'm very grateful.'

'There's nothing to be grateful for,' Angelo said.

'Yes, there is,' Muffin said. 'As you know full well.'


Bernard helped Rosetta carry the drinks back to Jenny and Marie, who had seen the developing action from their seats. They were ready as Rosetta introduced her new friend to them. 'This is Bernard,' Rosetta said. 'He's reading chemical engineering and he's from Shrewsbury.'

'I'm Marie, and this is Jenny.'

'Where are you both from, originally?' Bernard said.

'Bath,' Marie said.

'Originally?' Jenny said, accepting the question as her cue. 'I was made in heaven, and I'm planning to become a priest.'

Bernard took the lie in his stride. 'Anglican or Roman Catholic?'

'Oh, Roman Catholic,' Jenny said. 'I don't think there's any point in a woman becoming a priest if she's not willing to go all the way.'

Jenny and Marie began to laugh. Bernard smiled at Rosetta. Rosetta thought, he has a rather nice smile. And he seems to like me. She smiled back.

Marie said, 'Did Rosetta tell you what she does?'

'A nurse,' Bernard said. 'It's an undervalued profession.'

'No,' Marie said. 'What she *does*?'

'What do you *do*?' Bernard asked Rosetta easily.

'It's . . . I work in a vasectomy clinic,' Rosetta said.

'Oh,' Bernard said.

'They're teaching her how to *do* it,' Marie said.

'She's come up here to find some students to practise on,' Jenny said.


'You see,' Gina said to David, 'a professional burglar would have taken the money and some of the small silver things in the house. And an amateur burglar wouldn't have been able to get in without leaving signs of how he did it.'

161

'Can I have the mustard, please, Mum?'

'On chicken?'

'I'm in a mustard phase,' David said. 'I expect I'll grow out of it.'

Gina passed the mustard. 'So then I started talking with Charlie the way I do with your father, the way we do around the table. I said, "If he isn't a professional and if he isn't an amateur, maybe he isn't a burglar." Pass the salt, please.'

David passed the salt.


The Union bar filled rapidly and it wasn't long before another man approached the three women sitting alone by the window. Jenny saw him first. 'This one looks creepy,' she said to Marie. 'He's all yours.'

'Remind me to do *you* a favour sometime,' Marie said.

This man was a few years older than Bernard. He carried a bottle of beer but no glass. He dropped heavily on to the seat Bernard had vacated.

'Don't you wait till you're invited?' Marie said.

With a slimy smile the man said, 'I saw the guy who was here a few minutes ago.'

'Congratulations,' Jenny said. 'When did the surgeons restore your sight?'

'He ran out. What's the matter? You girls got Aids?'

'Yes,' Marie said. 'But you can't have any.'

'He was an atheist,' Jenny said.

Rosetta said nothing. She was looking at the man's knobbly hands.

'I'm not a student,' the man said. He fumbled in one of the pockets of his black mac. He pulled out a photograph. 'I'm a private detective. I'm trying to crack a tough case. Have any of you dames ever seen this broad?'


Gina said, 'So Charlie said, "If not a burglar then what?" So I said, "How about someone he already knew? Someone he would let into the house?" And Charlie said, "And there was a disagreement and that's why the old guy got hit?" And I said, "Maybe the guns were only taken to make it look like a burglary."'

David said, 'And then the guns were dumped?'

'Which would explain why they haven't turned up.'

'Is there any cheese?' David asked.


Jenny said, 'You're a private detective?'

'That's right,' Howard said. 'A genuine private eye.'

'Well, what a coincidence. So is my friend Marie here.'

Howard stared at Marie, obviously surprised. He opened his mouth. When eventually a word came out the word was, 'Bull.'

'No, it's true,' Jenny insisted, abandoning Marie's lie for a version of the truth. 'In fact Marie was working on a case only this afternoon, weren't you?'

Howard continued to stare at Marie, his jaw hanging loose.

'Yeah, she is gorgeous, isn't she,' Jenny said. 'Go on, Marie. Flutter your eyelashes for the nice man.'

Marie, well rum-and-coked, fluttered her eyelashes.

'Ain't those bitchin' eye-trims?' Jenny said.

'You may be pretty,' Howard said, 'but I bet you don't work on dangerous cases like I do.'

Marie said, 'I bet I do.'

'Tell about the case you were on today,' Jenny invited.

'Well,' Marie said, 'two men were trying to kill this other man, but we – that's the detective agency I work for – we're giving him round-the-clock protection, no matter what the expense.'

'That doesn't sound very dangerous.'

'More dangerous than showing people a picture.'

'Well,' Howard said, 'finding her's only the start.'

'Sounds more like the finish to me,' Marie said, tossing her hair. She laughed, like she laughed at David.

Howard didn't like it. 'You may protect people,' he said, 'but I bet you've never killed anybody.'

'Oh, and I suppose you have,' Jenny said.

'Could be,' Howard said.

'Yeah!' Marie said. 'We really believe that! And I bet the stain on your shirt is a bloodstain.'

Howard looked down at his shirt. There was no stain. The two girls laughed and hugged each other.

'You're taking the piss,' he said, growing angrier. 'But you shouldn't mess with me. I have killed someone.' He glared at one giggling girl, then the other. 'I have.'

David said, 'Is there any ice cream?'

'I think so,' Gina said. 'Maybe Howard was on the fiddle and it showed up in Block Letter's accounts.'

'And there was a showdown,' David said as he removed a container from the freezing compartment. 'And Howard smashed his head in.'

'Some of the quiet ones get violent when they're angry,' Gina said.

David spooned ice cream into a bowl. 'That plays,' he said solemnly.

'I drive a Jag,' Howard said.

'A Matchbox Jag?' Marie said. She and Jenny giggled. Rosetta watched.

Howard fumbled in his pockets. He pulled out a set of keys and waved them. 'I do!' he said. 'A real Jag, and it's great. I've had it customized. It's got a sensuous interior.'

'But no engine!' Marie said.

'Come out and see,' Howard said. 'I'll take you for a ride.'

'*Me?*' Marie said. 'Go for a ride in a car with *you?*'

'Why not?' Howard said.

'Get a life.'

'Honest, it's great,' Howard said. 'You'd like it.'

'I bet he doesn't even have a Jag,' Jenny said.

'Any more than he ever murdered somebody,' Marie said. She turned to Howard. 'Honestly! You're so full of shit it's coming out of your ears.'

'I never said "murdered",' Howard said.

164

'See?' Marie said.

'I just said "killed". It wasn't like I jumped out of a dark alley or anything. It was more an accident.' Suddenly he dropped his eyes, as if struck by an unpleasant memory. He played with the keys in his hands.

The three women glanced at each other, reacting to what seemed suddenly to be a core of truth.

Quietly Rosetta said, 'How did it happen?'

Howard said nothing.

Marie said, 'Was it self-defence, or what?'

'Go on,' Jenny said. 'I bet if you tell her she'll go for a ride in your Jag.'

Nobody laughed. For a moment nobody spoke. Then Howard looked up at Marie. 'Would you?'

'I might,' Marie said.

'It was no big deal,' Howard said with a jerky shrug. 'I was working at this place, and the boss was an old bloke, but he got at me all the time. Nothing I ever did was right. And then he said he wanted to see me, and he accused me of some stuff and it was all lies but he just wouldn't listen and so I kind of hit him. With a piece of wood. And I found out later he died.'

'There was a piece of wood handy?' Jenny said.

'It was the stock of a gun. There were some old guns around,' Howard said.

The three women were silent as they absorbed what they had been told.

'So,' Howard said to Marie, 'are you going to come for a ride with me? Or are you chicken?'

# 18

When the telephone rang, Gina answered it immediately.

Charlie said, 'I certainly didn't expect to be talking to you *again* today. I have this recurrent dream. There I am, sitting at home, my feet up, maybe watching a film on the tele. But each time I wake up and I'm still at work.'

'What's happened?' Gina said. 'Has Varden talked to Howard?'

'Howard's nowhere to be found,' Charlie said. 'This is about something else altogether.'

'What?'

'Gina, do you know where your children are?' Charlie asked.

'My children?' Gina looked at David, who was watching her across the kitchen table. 'David's here. Has something happened to Marie?'

'Not those children,' Charlie said. 'I mean your other children. Your older children.'

'I don't understand,' Gina said. Then, 'It's not Angelo, is it?'

'Worse,' Charlie said. 'I've got your in-laws down here.'


All three women accompanied Howard to the university car-park. 'See,' he said. 'It is a Jag. I told you.'

'So it is,' Jenny said.

'You didn't believe me,' Howard said.

'I'm impressed,' Marie said. 'It's good. Isn't it, Auntie Rose?'

Rosetta's *joie de vivre* had floated farther away with each successive rum and coke. As with the wine two nights before, the higher her blood alcohol got, the more bitter she became about Walter. And now, his *message*. Rosetta had no interest in anybody's Jag. So she said nothing.

'Shall we get in?' Howard said to Marie.

'OK.'

He could hardly believe it. He fumbled at the car door with his keys. 'Great!' he said.

'But only if my friends come too,' Marie said.


Gina offered to drive to the station to collect Mama and the Old Man but Charlie said he would drop them off on his way home. 'Home,' he repeated. 'Such an unfamiliar word . . .'

But in the event Charlie came up for a cup of coffee and to

166

recount the extraordinary behaviour of Gina's in-laws. 'I couldn't believe it,' he said. 'I had my jacket on. I had my briefcase in my hand. And then I get this call from downstairs.'

'Who else should we call?' the Old Man said.

'I'm not complaining, Mr Lunghi,' Charlie said. 'I'm just saying I was surprised. When was the last time you or Mrs Lunghi was in a police station?'

'Those terrible boys were breaking in,' Mama said. 'To steal. They were criminals.'

'What boys?' David said.

Charlie said, 'Two lads saw that the door at this Block Letter place had been forced. They went home to get their van and came back to cart away whatever they could load into it. Shows a bit more initiative than most of them have. Your common or garden opportunist doesn't go home for the van. But they certainly didn't bargain for the likes of these two.'

'But what were you doing at Block Letter?' Gina asked Mama and the Old Man.

'Not at,' Charlie said. 'In. They were inside.'

Gina looked from the Old Man to Mama.

Charlie said, 'These two malefactors were the ones who forced the door in the first place. They only told me that on the ride here.'

'To you, Charlie, we should tell the truth,' the Old Man said.

'Don't blame me,' Mama said. 'It was not my idea.'

'They got a come-uppance, the two hooligans,' the Old Man said with tired pride.

To Gina Charlie said, 'What your in-laws told the booking sergeant was that they were walking past the open door and thought the lads were behaving suspiciously. The one they captured kept saying, "They was inside already!" but of course nobody believed him.'

'You *captured* someone?' David said.

'He was a thief,' Mama said. 'And I didn't hit so hard he should make all that noise.'

'The other one ran,' Charlie said, 'but we have the van owner in custody. Your avenging in-laws caught up with him while he was trying to get it started.'

'Needs a service,' the Old Man said.

'Even if he got away,' Mama said, 'we saw his registration number.'

'So you didn't have to hit,' the Old Man said.

'Easy to say now,' Mama said.

'This one we got will rat on the other,' the Old Man said. 'You can tell.'

'Who got?' Mama said.

Gina said, 'But you didn't answer my question. What were you doing at Block Letter?'

'Ah,' the Old Man said. 'You got the papers?'

Mama took a sheaf of documents from her handbag. 'What do you think? I dropped them?'

'African,' the Old Man said. 'Like Shayler told us.'

'Shayler?' Gina said. 'As in our client?'

'Oh, by the way, Mum,' David said, 'Mr and Mrs Shayler came to consult us this afternoon.'

'They what?'

'Grandad took them up to the flat,' David said.

'Why didn't you tell me, David?' Gina said.

'I meant to. Sorry.'

'Is there anything else you want to tell me?'

'Listen,' the Old Man said. 'Nobody tells her anything. Now she knows what it's like.'

'For instance,' Gina said, 'does anybody know where Angelo is? And what he's up to with Muffin?'


Angelo got off the train tired but satisfied. He went down the stairs and through the underpass and it wasn't until he had emerged in front of the station that he began to think again about what he should say to Salvatore. Not to mention Gina. He crossed at the lights and headed toward home.

As he walked along the side of the bus station, a car squealed to a halt behind him. He turned to the sound and saw the car was a Jaguar. He stopped to admire it. One of the older models. Now *that* was a car.

As Angelo watched, the Jag's passenger door opened and a

168

young woman backed out, bending into the car's interior. In a moment Angelo could see why. The first young woman – who put him in mind of Marie – helped a second young woman out. This one, in turn, helped a third.

The third woman was Rosetta. And, yes, the first woman *was* Marie. Angelo set off toward the Jaguar. 'Marie! Rosetta!'

As Angelo drew close he heard a weedy male voice say, 'But you *promised* you'd come out with me again.'

'I didn't say *when!*' Marie said. 'Don't call me. I'll call you.' She slammed the passenger door. The three women moved away from the car at a trot.

'Marie?' Angelo said.

'Dad!' Marie said. 'We're just going to the chipper before Jenny catches her bus. We're starving!'

'Hi, Mr Lunghi!' Jenny said.

Behind Marie, Jenny and Rosetta Angelo saw the driver of the Jaguar open his door and begin to emerge. 'Marie, who is that in the car?'

'He says he's Clint,' Marie said.

Jenny giggled. After a moment's delay, Rosetta laughed too, loudly.

'Auntie Rose is pissed,' Marie said.

'I'm pissed,' Rosetta said. 'Pissed as a newt.'

The Jaguar driver saw the three women talking to Angelo. He got back in his car, revved his engine, and screeched away.

'Newt, newt,' Rosetta said.

'But he's really *Howard!*' Marie said.

'Howard?' Angelo said. 'Howard the Printer?' He looked after the Jag.

'Tonight he was Howard the Detective,' Marie said.

'Newt,' Rosetta said.

'He fancies Marie,' Jenny said.

'Who does?' Angelo said.

'Howard does!' Marie said. 'He gave me his home phone number and everything. And he told us the most amazing story!'

'Walter,' Rosetta said. 'Walter.'

'What?' Angelo said.

'Walter is a newt,' Rosetta said. 'He says he's going to have it reversed. But I don't want his baby, Angelo. I don't want it. I'm too young. Besides, someone else is coming to lunch tomorrow. So you tell Gina, I don't want Walter's baby. OK?'

# 19

'It wasn't a real murder,' the Old Man said.

'I bet the dead man doesn't agree with you, Papa,' Salvatore said.

'Will you have some spaghetti, Mr White?' Mama asked. 'Shall I put some on your plate?'

'Yes, thank you. And, please, my friends call me Iggy,' Ignatius White said.

'And some sauce, Iggy?' Mama said. 'It's got mussels, my own recipe.'

'Wonderful.'

'I mean it wasn't a real murder *case*,' the Old Man said. 'Not with surveillance and investigation and routine and detail.'

'I'm sure the police did plenty of that,' Salvatore said.

'But *we* didn't,' the Old Man said. 'That's the point.'

'Are they going to arrest him?' Marie asked.

'They may already have done it,' Gina said. 'Charlie said they were going to his house this morning.'

'Oooh, poor Howard,' Marie said.

'But he's awful, Marie!' Rosetta said. 'So smirky, and full of himself, and think what he did to that poor man.' Rosetta shivered.

'We must remain mindful of the victim, is what I say,' Ignatius White said.

'But think,' Marie said. 'He woke up this morning and thought it was just another day. He went down to have breakfast with his mother planning to tell her all about the gorgeous women he had in his car last night. And suddenly, there's a knock at the door! Who can it be at this time on a Sunday? And even then he doesn't have the slightest hint that his whole world is about to crumble.'

'Some world,' the Old Man said.

'It can't be helped,' Angelo said. 'Solve one person's problem, and you make a problem for the next.'

'That's a bit philosophical,' Gina said.

'Maybe I'm in the wrong business,' Angelo said.

'Maybe it should be the knight in shining armour business,' Gina suggested.

'What could I do?' Angelo asked.

'I made the broccoli with almonds, Iggy,' Rosetta said.

'It's delicious,' Ignatius White said. 'Everything is delicious, truly. But the broccoli is specially commended. Might I have some more?'

Mama's eyes shone as she passed the broccoli. 'So tell me, Iggy,' she said, 'what do you do for a living?'

'At the moment I install computers. But I'm moving into sales.'

'Not a lawyer, then?' the Old Man said.

'More Parmesan?' Mama said abruptly. 'That's not enough.'

'It's plenty,' the Old Man said. 'Is it supposed to be a blanket?' After a moment he sprinkled another spoonful of Parmesan over his spaghetti.

'That's how I met your lovely daughter, the computers,' Ignatius White said.

'And Iggy is going to save us lots of money,' Rosetta said.

'Money?' the Old Man said.

'How's that, Rose?' Angelo asked.

'You know all this new equipment we have on trial?'

'On trial?' Angelo said. 'I thought we bought it.'

'Noooo, silly! I haven't signed anything,' Rosetta said. 'But Iggy knows how we can get it cheaper.'

'Nothing fraudulent, I hope,' Angelo said. 'Not that I'm accusing you of dishonesty,' he added quickly. 'It's just that we have an investigation that has suddenly become a large fraud case.'

'We?' the Old Man said to Mama. 'He says "We"? So where is he when the Shaylers want to consult?'

171

'Yes, Angelo,' Gina said quietly, 'do tell us what you were up to yesterday while the rest of us were capturing thieves in their vans, gathering evidence for fraud cases, and solving murders.'

'I heard that,' the Old Man said. 'And it wasn't a murder. Not a real murder.'

'He hears when he wants to hear,' Mama said to Gina, shaking her head.

'Are the African documents you brought home last night the fraud evidence, Grandma?' David asked.

'That's right,' Mama said.

'All for companies that don't exist,' the Old Man said. 'Order forms, invoice forms, receipt forms, and not one company is real. Not one.'

'Is it against the law to print forms for fake companies?' David asked.

'You can print what you like,' the Old Man said.

'So what's the fraud?'

'When you go to the bank to borrow money because you're doing such wonderful business in Africa, that's the fraud. Huh!'

Angelo said, 'If you use the documents to pretend you have assets, and then borrow money on those assets.'

'Like,' David said, 'if we borrowed money on our new computers, but they aren't really ours?'

'That's the idea,' Angelo said. 'Only with this case the idea was probably to borrow a lot of money and then abscond to a country where there's no extradition and live in luxury.'

'Can anybody do that?' Marie asked.

'Not stupid people who get low GCSEs,' David said.

Marie smacked David's arm. 'They were just mocks, as you know perfectly well.'

'A fraud case, that's what it is,' the Old Man said. '*Not* murder.'

'How much money was involved?' Salvatore asked.

'No telling until they go through the details,' Gina said.

'No fun sorting all that out,' Salvatore said.

'I wondered if maybe they'll get Mr Shayler to do it,' Gina said.

'Fun?' the Old Man said. 'Work has to be fun? When did they make a law? Huh!'

'Go on, Papa,' Salvatore said. 'Are you telling me you didn't get a kick out of breaking into Block Letter? Because if you tell me that, I won't believe you.'

'A son should believe his father,' the Old Man said, but he could not help grinning.

'See,' Salvatore said. 'What he is at heart is a ram raider.'

'Someone had to do it,' the Old Man said. 'With nobody else around.' He rubbed the shoulder that broke Block Letter's door open. 'Pepper. Where's the pepper?'

'Here it is, Grandad!' Marie said brightly, passing the pepper.

Gina said, 'Sally, I thought you were going to bring someone to lunch?'

'She couldn't come,' Salvatore said. 'She had to work.'

'Work?' Mama said. 'She's a tourist.'

'It's not Muffin, Mama. This is a girl called Cheryl.'

'Cheryl?' Mama asked. 'But – '

'I don't know what's happened to Muffin,' Salvatore said. 'She just vanished.'

'Don't be silly,' Mama said. 'Muffins don't vanish.'

'Angelo knows about Muffin,' Gina said.

'Do you, bubba?'

'Angelo?' Mama said.

'Muffin went home,' Angelo said.

'Home?' Mama said. 'What do you mean, home?'

'Back to America, Mama.'

'Why would she do that?' Mama said. She frowned deeply. 'So sudden. Salvatore?'

'I don't know anything about it,' Salvatore said.

'Muffin flew back to America yesterday,' Angelo said. 'She's trying to sort out a difficult personal problem.'

'What personal problem?' Mama demanded. 'Salvatore, why does Angelo know all about this nice girl?'

Angelo said, 'Muffin needed to go back to America, but she was afraid and nervous, so I went to the airport with her.'

'Why was she afraid?' Mama said. 'What did Salvatore do to upset her so much?'

'I know you liked her, Mama,' Salvatore said. 'I liked her too. But I don't know anything about it.'

'It was nothing to do with Salvatore,' Angelo said. 'She had a different problem altogether. Truly, Mama.'

Mama sighed. Could there be a more difficult problem than Salvatore? And if he's always going to disappoint, why bring them to the house at all? Why torment a mother so? Mama said nothing.

'Is Muffin really gone forever, Dad?' David asked.

Angelo nodded.

'But she was going to teach me things on the computer.'

'And she owes *me* money,' Marie said. 'Ten quid.'

'So what's this new one you got?' the Old Man asked. 'Another doctor?'

'No, Papa,' Salvatore said with a laugh.

'A lawyer, maybe? To support you with her income?' But before the Old Man could develop either a legal or a financial theme, the door bell rang. 'Is somebody expecting?' the Old Man asked. He looked around his family.

Rosetta said, 'Not me, Papa.'

Salvatore got up. 'I'll see who it is.' He left the room.

'Does anybody know who it can be?' Gina said.

'It doesn't matter as long as they pay,' the Old Man said.

Everybody laughed except Ignatius White. The Old Man said, 'What's funny?' As he did so, the telephone rang. 'And now the telephone? What is this? Who rings?'

Angelo rose and went to the nearest phone, which was in the kitchen.

'Excuse me,' Ignatius White said.

'Yes, Iggy?' Mama said. 'Some more broccoli? More sauce? Look at him. He wants building up.'

'You were just talking about someone who had promised to teach David about the new computers.'

'That's right,' Mama said sweetly.

'Well, if David would like some instruction, I can probably help.'

'There you go, brain-drain,' Marie said.

'That's very generous of you, Iggy,' Gina said. 'Isn't that kind, David?'

174

David looked across the table at Ignatius White.

'I'd be pleased, delighted to help you, David,' Ignatius White said.

David managed to say, 'Thank you.'

Angelo appeared from the kitchen. 'Marie. For you.'

Marie jumped up and closed the door behind her father as Angelo returned to his seat.

'Who rings people in the middle of Sunday lunch?' the Old Man asked.

'This call,' Angelo said deliberately, 'was from a classmate of Marie's named Terry. He says he wants to talk to her about a band called Easy Money.'

Before anyone could comment Salvatore reappeared. He carried a cage. 'For Gina,' he said.

'What for does Gina want a birdcage?' the Old Man asked.

'For her canary,' Salvatore said, pointing to a tiny, pale lemon bird with black markings perched in a corner.

'For me?' Gina said.

'From an old guy with braces,' Salvatore said. 'He said he was a friend of yours. He said he knew how much you must be missing Jasper.'

'The Shaylers' neighbour,' Gina said.

'Your friend says he's sorry Patch isn't orange like Jasper, but he's sure Patch is male and that he'll be a good singer. Keep the cage as long as you need it. And if you want to drop in, he has some bird books you might find interesting. To tell the truth, Gina,' Salvatore said, 'I think the old guy's in love with you.'

Gina buried her face in her hands.

'You going to satisfy this customer?' Salvatore asked.

'The Shaylers,' the Old Man said to Ignatius White. 'Satisfied clients. But definitely *not* a murder case.'

'How interesting,' Ignatius White said.

'Now Norman Stiles, *that* was a murder case.'

From around the table groans arose. Ignatius White did not understand them at all.